an Intern Diaries novella

FROM EUGENE WITH LOVE

DC GOMEZ

With love,
DC Gomez

ISBN: 978-1-7333160-1-9
Published by Gomez Expeditions
Request to publish work from this book should be sent to:
author@dcgomez-author.com

OTHER BOOKS BY D. C. GOMEZ

URBAN FANTASY:

Death's Intern- Book 1 in the Intern Diaries Series
Plague Unleashed- Book 2 in the Intern Diaries Series
Forbidden War- Book 3 in the Intern Diaries Series
The Origins of Constantine- an Intern Diary Novella

YOUNG ADULT:

Another World- Book 1 in the Another World Trilogy

WOMEN'S LITERATURE:

The Cat Lady Special

AND A CHILDREN'S SERIES – CHARLIE'S FABLE:

Charlie, what's your talent? - Book 1
Charlie, dare to dream! – Book 2

TABLE OF CONTENTS

This book is for all the dreamers in this world.
May you always reach for the stars.

CHAPTER 1

It was an unusually cool morning for July in the southwest corner of Arkansas—only sixty degrees. Normally by this time of the year, the temperature would be at least seventy-five degrees by seven a.m. According to the locals, one should expect a hot summer since the winter was so mild. Eugene was not complaining. He loved this mild weather. In reality, Eugene loved all the seasons. Anytime he could spend a day outside away from the lab was a great day for him.

Eugene was the Rookie Intern for Pestilence, who was one of the four Horsemen of the Apocalypse. She had a horrible reputation with everyone outside the lab. Pestilence was dominating, arrogant, and sometimes condescending, but she truly loved her Interns. Even if she made them call her Mistress and referred to them by numbers…

The newest member of the team was always the Rookie. After ten years on the job, if they made it that far, they graduated to First, ten years later to Second and so on until Ninth. Pestilence always had ten Interns serving her. Eugene was excited to be recruited since he was the first black male in over one-hundred years to have the job.

Eugene learned very early on the job that the Rookie always had the worst assignments. He didn't care. He was living his dream as a scientist in the most advanced lab in the world. Anything he could imagine, he had the resources to create. That was the reason he was standing in the middle of a field in Fulton, Arkansas watching honey bees at seven in the morning.

"Rookie. One more time, tell me why we are here and not heading towards the Coliseum?" Fourth asked Eugene for the fifth time in less than ten minutes.

"We are checking the status of my honey bees so we can transport them back to the lab." Eugene repeated the same answer he had given Fourth five times already.

"Right, but why now?" Fourth asked, clearly not giving up.

"I always check my bees on the way to the club," Eugene admitted.

Eugene wasn't technically doing anything against any of the rules they had. He was still doing Pestilence's work, just making a little detour to run his own experiments before he delivered her goods.

The Interns were responsible for manufacturing drugs for Pestilence's underground rave club in Texarkana. Pestilence's lab was located in Hope, Arkansas, underneath a chicken plant. The lab was less than an hour away from Texarkana, which made it an easy drive. Eugene and Fourth were carrying over one-hundred pounds of straight heroin, methamphetamine, and amphetamine to be diluted in the club to make Ecstasy. They had a huge order due to Pestilence for her upcoming Fourth of July Bash in two days.

"Hanging out with Death's people is making you radical," Fourth finally said after staring at Eugene for a long time. "I'm going to nap. Let me know when you are ready to leave." Fourth didn't wait for a reply. Instead, he started toward the company car: a hearse.

Eugene raised his voice. "Aren't you going to help me?"

"Rookie, I like your spunk and initiative," Fourth replied with a huge grin. "Turning honey bees to killer ones, and releasing them back to their environment is brilliant. I'm your man when you bring them back to the lab. But I'm not going to crawl around in a field watching bees. That's rookie work. Have fun and don't delay," Fourth told Eugene as he walked away.

Eugene just shook his head. Fourth was a brilliant scientist with a background in biogenetic. He was always ahead of his time, but he also liked to sleep and his famous naps lasted hours. Eugene gave up any hope of Fourth helping him catalogue to prepare for the move.

Moving bees was a tricky business. To safely relocate them, the move should be done at night. At least that was one of the theories Eugene had heard from the local bee-keepers in Texarkana. He never imagined he would find a group of bee-keepers in this area.

A screeching noise drew his attention, and he turned around just in time to see a couple of men climb into the hearse and slam the doors. He ran for the car, but rocks flew at him from the gravel as they zoomed away. The exhaust pipe popped from the exertion, and Eugene jumped at the sound. Eugene couldn't believe it, the hearse, the drugs, and Fourth were gone.

"Oh God," Eugene mumbled to himself. "I'm so dead." He dropped his forehead into his palm. What was he going to do?

Eugene started pacing back and forth. He tried to think of a way to fix this, but his brain had shut down. Next, his mouth went dry, and then his palms started to sweat. He was stranded in the middle of a field in Arkansas. He couldn't call the lab because they would kill him.

No, there was only one person he could call right now that would help him without a single judgment. He pulled his cell phone out and dialed.

"Hello," answered a male voice from the receiver.

"Hi Bob. It's me, Eugene," Eugene squeaked out.

"Hey Eugene, what's going on?" Bob asked.

The horsemen Interns and their staff didn't used to get along. Things changed after the incident in May when a disgruntled accountant that used to work for Pestilence set off a zombie plague in the Twin cities of Texarkana. Death convinced Pestilence to let Eugene join her team every weekend and he loved those trips. It got him out of the underground lab for a little while.

"I have a small problem," Eugene told Bob, not sure how to break the news to his friend that he lost another case of dangerous substances.

"What's going on? Are you okay?" Bob asked.

"I'm kind of stranded at my field of bees. Could you pick me up?" Eugene decided it was probably safer to tell Bob face to face.

"Do I want to know what happened?" Bob asked.

"I will tell you when I get to Reapers," Eugene told Bob.

"Okay. I'll send Shorty to pick you up," Bob said.

"Is this a punishment? You don't even know what I did," Eugene told Bob, his words rushing from his mouth. His stomach was turning, and he was sure he was going to pass out any minute.

"Of course it is not a punishment. Shorty just happens to be closer to you. Unless you want to be standing in the middle of a field for at least thirty minutes," Bob told Eugene.

Eugene weighed his options. He could stay in the field and wait for Bob or risk his life at the hands of Mad-Max Shorty. If it wasn't for Fourth being taken in that hearse, he would stay in the field. But his friend's life could be in danger, so he really had no other options.

Eugene let out a heavy sigh. "Fine, send Shorty. But if I don't make it, I'm blaming you."

"He is already on his way. Stop being dramatic. You will be fine. Just remember to put on your seatbelt," Bob told Eugene with a hint of amusement in his voice. "See you in a bit."

"You might, but only if I don't die on the way," Eugene told the optimistic Bob.

In less than seven minutes, a huge Ford Truck charged straight at Eugene. Unable to move, he knew he must look like a deer stuck in headlights. Finally, at the last second, he pulled himself from his trance and jumped out of the way, landing flat on the ground right as the truck stopped in the exact spot Eugene had just been standing. The driver side door opened and Shorty jumped out, walking over to Eugene.

"E, my man, why are you on the ground?" Shorty asked.

"I swear you do this on purpose to scare the hell out of people," Eugene told Shorty.

Shorty laughed and offered Eugene his hand. Shaking his head, Eugene accepted it and dragged himself off the ground. He brushed his now dirt-covered clothing, trying to making himself presentable, but his attempt failed miserably.

Next to Shorty, Eugene looked like a giant. Even though he stood at only five-foot-nine, Shorty was barely five-four and maybe one-hundred-and-twenty pounds fully dressed. The man was tiny, but like dynamite, he was a force to be reckoned with.

"Come on E, do you really think I would do that?" Shorty asked, the hint of smirk brushing the corners of his lips.

Eugene crinkled his eyebrows. Shorty's attempt to hide his smile told him that he had definitely done it on purpose. Just for good measure, he said, "Yes you would." Then he went back to trying to clean his coat.

"Do you always wear your bath robe to the field?" Shorty asked.

"It is not a bath robe. It's my lab coat and it's the standard uniform of Pestilence's Interns." Eugene gave up brushing his coat as he finished talking. "Oh never mind. Let's get this over with."

"Great. I have a meeting with the triplets at I-Hop and I don't want to miss it," Shorty told Eugene as he ran around the truck. "Where is your corpse-mobile? I know you didn't walk here."

Eugene let out another sigh. "Stolen," he said as he climbed in the truck.

"What?" Shorty yelled. "Why didn't you say that before? We

been sitting here losing time. You need to talk to Boss Man. He will know what to do." Shorty started the truck before Eugene buckled his seatbelt.

Eugene hoped that Death's team could help, but more than anything, he dreaded facing one specific member of the team. Isis Black was Death's North American Intern and one of the most beautiful women Eugene had ever seen. She was tall with silky black hair and a mocha complexion. She was also extremely intelligent and lethal. In fact, he had a feeling Isis could beat him up with one hand. However, even with all her badassery, Isis was also one of the most caring people he knew, and the last thing he wanted to do was disappoint her. This was going to suck.

Before Eugene could drown himself in his sorrow, Shorty took off. Eugene had just enough time to grab the oh-shit handle before he took the fastest turn in the history of driving.

"Shorty, don't get me killed. I'm too young to die!" Eugene screamed, although he had a feeling Shorty still couldn't hear him. The music was so loud it almost blew out his eardrums.

"Relax E. I got this," Shorty said.

Eugene shrugged. He guessed Shorty had heard him after all.

CHAPTER 2

Reapers Incorporated was located at the Nash Business Park in Nash, Texas. Needless to say, Eugene and Shorty made it there in record time. That was the fastest drive to Nash that Eugene had ever witnessed—especially from the passenger's seat. Eugene could feel his heart racing in his chest. He took his heartbeat and by the time they arrived, his heart rate was over one-hundred-and-twenty beats per minute and his hands were shaking. Eugene was sure he was having a panic attack, but was it any wonder when Shorty's idea of a good time was cutting in front of eighteen-wheelers and driving faster than a State-Trooper on a chase?

Eugene's life at the lab hadn't prepared him for Shorty's driving.

Reapers was the headquarters of Death's team. From the outside, the building looked like every other metal building on the business complex. The only distinct characteristic was the red gothic letters on the name, which Eugene was sure had been ordered by Constantine.

Constantine was the guardian for all of Death's Interns, as well as their trainer. He was also a five-thousand-year-old talking cat. Eugene hadn't known such things existed. He wasn't used to the supernatural world, and even though he knew it was there, he had very little interaction with it. Until he met Death's group.

Eugene and Shorty were part of the team at Reapers, according to Bartholomew. Bartholomew was the resident genius of the group and was only twelve. His duties ranged from hacker, supply sergeant, and occasionally even arms dealer. To expedite their visits, Bartholomew had programmed the security system to recognize both Shorty and Eugene's handprint and DNA, which saved a lot of time since Reapers had more security than Fort Knox.

Once Eugene and Shorty scanned their hands on the small electronic pad next to the door, they moved inside the building and walked through the scanning system. Bartholomew once explained that the system looked for everything, including spells, arms, and even food. Eugene was not sure how the food one applied, but he was afraid to ask. Death's team had strange reasons for doing stuff.

They made it through the security tunnel, as Eugene referred to it, and crossed the first floor of the building, which was a lot more impressive on the inside. It was set up in sections. Bob had his apartment next to the tunnel at the front of the building. The middle was split between a gym and the parking/maintenance area for their cars. Eugene glanced over as he passed, whispering a quick prayer of thanks when he noticed the blue Mini Cooper that belonged to Isis wasn't there. The back of the first floor doubled as a shooting range and lab. That was the place Eugene usually confiscated when he needed to work.

The building had a second floor on the far end. The loft, as Isis called it, was the living quarters for the rest of the team. The front of the loft had an impressive kitchen that Bob claimed for himself, which was fine with everybody since he was the master chef. The rest of the loft housed Bartholomew's command center and a dining room set. Eugene could see the loft from the first floor since the inside wall was made of glass.

"Are you planning to stay down here all day?" Shorty asked Eugene.

"I'm not sure I'm ready to face them," Eugene admitted in a soft tone.

"Oh come on E, we are family," Shorty told him. "Yes, Boss Man is going to make fun of you, but Constantine makes fun of everyone. Now relax and let's get your corpse-mobile back." Shorty flashed a confident smile and headed up the stairs.

Eugene searched the room for a way out, but when he couldn't find one, he sucked it up and followed.

When Shorty entered the loft, Eugene trailed behind him with his shoulders slumped. He stopped and scanned the room, finding Bartholomew sitting in front of his command station and Constantine napping on top of the leather couch. Bob, of course, was in the kitchen area.

Bob was Eugene's favorite. He was only in his forties, but very wise for his age. Whenever Eugene needed someone to talk to, Bob listened and gave great advice. He'd kind of become Eugene's mentor, which made this even harder. What if Bob was disappointed in him?

"Boss Man, we made it," Shorty told Constantine.

Constantine yawned and opened his eyes. Then he stretched for what felt like five minutes, taking his Sphinx pose on top of the couch. Finally, he gave them a bored look. "Shorty, you're slacking. What happened? I was expecting you here at least ten minutes ago."

"Sorry Boss Man," Shorty answered, fidgeting with his shirt. Eugene wondered if Shorty was embarrassed. "I was afraid E would puke in the truck." He gave Eugene a side glance.

"Good call," Bob added. "The smell of puke would never come out." Bob winked at Eugene. "Have a seat, Eugene. You look a little pale." Bob pointed towards the dining table.

Eugene dropped into one of the dining room chairs and waited for the lecture. Instead, everyone just stared at him. After a few awkward moments, Bob handed Eugene a plate of Huevos Rancheros.

"Thanks," Eugene mumbled.

"Everything looks better after a meal," Bob told him and went back to the kitchen for his coffee.

"I agree with Bob, but are you going to tell us what happened?" Constantine asked Eugene. "Why were you stranded at your bee field? By the way, have I mentioned your bee idea is nuts? Brilliant, but still nuts," Constantine told Eugene.

Eugene fiddled with the bottom of his coat while trying to build his courage. Before he knew it, he blurted out, "Somebody stole the hearse while I was checking on the bees."

"That's it?" Constantine asked. "You are looking this pathetic over the hearse. Why?" Constantine shook his head and mumbled something Eugene couldn't understand.

"Fourth was in the hearse when they stole it," Eugene added, barely able to stop himself from crying.

"What?" Shorty shouted. "He let himself get stolen?" He tried to cover his mouth to hide his smile, but he was too late.

"Fourth is a really heavy sleeper, and he was taking a nap in the back," Eugene tried to explain. "He is probably still asleep," Eugene said as he stabbed his eggs around his plate.

"I'm impressed. It takes talent to sleep that deep," Bob told Eugene.

"There is something seriously wrong with those Interns," Constantine told the group. "What's the problem again? When

Fourth wakes up he can walk out and call you," Constantine said in a straightforward tone.

"That's not the only thing missing," Eugene said, sliding down on his chair.

"I don't like the sound of that," Constantine said.

"We were carrying over one-hundred pounds of pure chemicals and cocaine to make Ecstasy." The words flew from his lips, coming so fast together he hoped they didn't understand what he'd just admitted. Except, he was never that lucky.

"What?" Constantine growled.

"Damn," Shorty added.

"Eugene, how potent are the chemicals you were carrying?" Bob asked, gripping the kitchen counter.

"Overdose strength," Eugene answered without meeting anyone's eyes.

"Have you told Pestilence yet?" Constantine asked, almost spitting Pestilence's name.

"I can't," Eugene said, his tone filled with panic. He jumped from his seat, ready to bolt. "We have strict rules when it comes to chemicals out of the lab. We aren't supposed to let them out of our sight. If anyone tries to take them, we're supposed to retaliate with a polio shot." Eugene paced the length of the room.

"What do you mean by polio shot?" Bob asked Eugene.

"We carried an EpiPen with it," Eugene answered as he stopped and looked at the floor. "Well we are supposed to, but I left mine in my bag inside the hearse."

"No wonder those poor Rotarians are still fighting polio when Pestilence has her people spreading it." Constantine shook his head. "Spill it, Eugene. What's the penalty for losing your chemicals?" Constantine asked Eugene.

Eugene picked at the dirt specks embedded in his coat and swallowed the lump in his throat. Any minute he might cry, and he couldn't have that in front of Death's crew. "How did you know?"

"With Pestilence, there is always a punishment. That witch is nuts," Constantine answered.

"A year of manual labor in the lower levels of the lab with no ability to see the sun," Eugene told the group.

"Ouch. E, you work in hell," Shorty told Eugene.

"I agree with Shorty. That is cruel." Bob rubbed his temple like he was trying to release all the stress inside him.

"It will be worse since I lost Fourth as well," Eugene finished, dropping back down in his chair.

"Relax, child. We will find your missing boy and your drugs before that psycho witch finds out," Constantine told him.

"Really?" Eugene asked, sitting straight up in his chair and smiling for the first time since arriving at Reapers.

"Of course," Constantine said. "We can't let her take our favorite mad-Scientist."

"Could you do me a favor and not tell Isis either?" Eugene asked.

"Why?" Shorty asked. "You know the Boss Lady is a huge asset," Shorty told Eugene.

"I don't want her to think I'm totally irresponsible," Eugene admitted.

"You don't care if *we* think you are totally irresponsible?" Constantine asked him in a teasing voice.

"You guys are my boys. You don't care if I am. Isis has high hopes for people. Especially me," Eugene almost whispered.

"He does have a point, Boss," Bob told Constantine.

"You are in luck since she's in Jefferson on a job," Constantine barely got out before the door busted open and Isis ran in.

"Hi, just here for a minute," Isis said, running into the loft. She stopped short when she saw Eugene. "Eugene, what are you doing here?" Isis asked.

"Delivering more sleep formula. He brought us the wrong one on Friday," Constantine answered for him. "The real question is, what are you doing here?" Constantine asked with a frown.

"Need to get some clothes," Isis answered, not looking at Constantine.

"What happened? Why do you need more clothes?" Bob said quickly.

"Nothing happened. It's just going to take me a little longer to track this ghost down," Isis answered, trying to smile.

"Are you sure?" Constantine asked. "Or are you trying to have a mini-vacation at a bed-and-breakfast?" Constantine narrowed his eyes towards Isis.

"Hanging out in a haunted hotel is work, not a vacation," Isis told him. "Nope, just having a hard time tracking his patterns. He keeps moving houses and I can't tell which ones are actually haunted by a ghost or if it is just humans pretending to be ghosts. But don't fear. I got this." Isis ran to the back of the loft towards the bedrooms.

"Why are you harassing her? We want her to go, don't we?" Eugene whispered to Constantine.

"Eugene, Isis's room is sound proof. You don't have to whisper. Besides, if I don't pick on her, she will know something is wrong," Constantine answered.

"Got it!" screamed Bartholomew from the back.

Eugene jumped in his seat. "Don't do that."

"Sorry about that," Bartholomew replied, taking off his head phones.

"It's about time," Constantine told him.

"Hey, it's not my fault Eugene doesn't have a tracker on his hearse," Bartholomew said, trying to defend himself. "I had to create a program to scan and track for hearses. Do you know how many hearses there are in this area? Tons." Bartholomew shook a finger at his screen.

"Wait, you found the hearse?" Eugene asked.

"What do you think I was doing here? Playing Pokémon?" Bartholomew replied in a sarcastic voice.

"Ignoring me," Eugene told him.

"You got jokes. Thanks, E," Bartholomew replied, using Shorty's nickname. "But we got a problem. I tracked it to the old Electric Cowboy."

"I thought that place was closed," Eugene added.

"It is to the public, but not the group that hangs there," Bob said, crossing his arms and shaking his head.

"Okay, who hangs out there?" Eugene asked.

"We are tracking a gang of werewolves in that location," Bartholomew told Eugene.

"Oh wow. This day just keeps getting better," Eugene answered, dropping back in his chair and putting his head on the table.

"In that case, I recommend you all hurry. We don't need the night crowd joining that bunch," Constantine told them. "Besides, better take off before Isis comes back out and starts asking questions." Constantine looked in the direction of the bedrooms.

"Shorty, you better join us. This could get ugly," Bob told Shorty.

Shorty, Eugene, and Bob left the loft in a hurry. Eugene's stomach turned like he might be sick any minute, but somehow, he kept moving. This was not at all how he'd expected his day to go.

CHAPTER 3

The Electric Cowboy used to be a popular club in Texarkana. It no longer functioned as a club, though, since the location was condemned. However, the building was still intact.

Bob and Eugene rode together in Bob's truck, which he called Storm. Shorty followed extremely close in his truck, and Eugene couldn't help but notice how Shorty's driving never quite affected Bob. Of course, he was prior military and served in Desert Storm, and Shorty's driving did simulate combat maneuvers.

"This place is deserted," Eugene told Bob as they pulled into the parking lot.

"That's a blessing. I doubt the three of us could handle a gang of werewolves," Bob replied as he parked next to the hearse. "Have you considered giving the hearse a paint job?" Bob asked Eugene, pointing at the rust spots littering the vehicle.

"We just did. Then Second tested a new formula on it and peeled half the paint job away," Eugene replied with a pout. What he didn't say was he was the one that had to paint the damn thing. "We are waiting for him to get past his chemical testing before painting it again." He rolled his eyes.

"That's some intense testing," replied Bob. "I don't blame you for waiting. But that poor hearse is looking rough." Bob shook his head. Eugene knew Bob really felt sorry for the company vehicle because he had a passion for cars—one Eugene would never understand.

Shorty jumped off his truck and rushed to the side of the building. Eugene and Bob climbed off Storm a lot slower. They made their way around the hearse, taking inventory.

"Everything is gone. I'm done," Eugene told Bob as he kicked rocks around like a sad child.

"Stop pouting, Eugene," Bob told him. "We will figure this out."

"Big Bob, I got some news," Shorty shouted as he was walked back with another guy.

"Hey Billy, how are you?" Bob asked the new guy.

"Hi Big Bob. Doing good, holding things down," Billy told Bob.

Billy was in his late twenties, around five-seven with dark hair and black eyes. He had on camouflage pants and a shirt that looked like it had seen better days. His average looks were perfect for blending in and being unrecognizable.

"Billy this is Eugene, the owner of the hearse," Bob said. "Billy is Shorty's latest recruit and one of our star pupils. We know he is going to do great things." Bob and Shorty both beamed like proud parents, smiling from ear to ear. Billy blushed from the compliment.

Eugene shook hands with Billy and realized his appearance was only for show. The man smelled like Axe body wash.

"A pleasure," Eugene told him.

"Did you see anything?" Bob asked Billy after introductions were concluded.

"It was weird," Billy said. "Two of the young ones pulled in the parking lot driving the hearse like bats out of hell, then two more followed in a Ford F-150. They were happier than a fat kid eating cake. I couldn't hear everything they were saying, but it sounded like they said they just won the jackpot and were going to teach the man a lesson." Billy looked at Eugene, who just shook his head, hoping to clarify that he wasn't "the man," but Billy started talking again. "Then out of the back of the hearse this guy wearing a white coat like Eugene's jumped out. Scared the hell out of everyone, too. The two young ones freaked out, and one of the guys from the truck hit him over the head."

"Oh no. They killed him!" Eugene screamed and started pacing a circle around the group.

"I'm pretty sure they didn't kill him," Billy told Eugene.

"You don't understand. Fourth is sensitive," Eugene tried to explain. "The man passed out from paper cuts."

"Oh. Well, in that case, he might be dead then," Billy agreed with Eugene. "Is his name really Fourth?" Billy asked, looking between Bob and Shorty for answers.

"Long story, my boy. And one you really don't want to know," Shorty told Billy, padding him on the shoulder as he turned to look around the place.

"I'm so dead," Eugene said in a high-pitched voice.

"Stop being dramatic. Nobody is going to die," Bob told Eugene. "Billy, where did they go?" Bob asked trying to hold Eugene from starting his new pacing marathon. Bob failed and Eugene was back to pacing.

"They didn't say, they just shoved the poor guy in the truck and took off," Billy answered.

"Have you seen anyone else around here?" Shorty asked. "This place looks like a cemetery, even for a Monday morning." Shorty's gaze roamed as he spoke.

"Lately, most of the gang clears the place between midnight and two," Billy told him. "The cops have been doing more regular check-ups in the area, so they are staying clear."

"When do they normally come back?" Bob asked him.

"Between four and six in the afternoon. I'm guessing some of them actually have jobs." Billy shoved his hands in his pockets and shrugged.

"Good job, Billy. Keep an eye on the place," Bob said.

"If they come back with the coat-man, give me a call," Shorty told him.

"Will do, Boss." Billy saluted both Shorty and Bob and took off. He waved at Eugene as he passed him.

"Now what?" Eugene asked, sounding like he was hyperventilating. Before he could add to his questions, his phone rang, which made him jump a foot off the ground.

"E, my man, you need to calm down before you give yourself a heart attack," Shorty told Eugene, shaking his head.

"Shorty is right. Calm down, Eugene." When Bob agreed with Shorty, Eugene knew he was in trouble.

"Hello." Eugene decided to answer the phone instead of arguing with the two men.

"Rookie, what is going on?" the man on the other line asked.

"Hi Seventh, what do you mean?" Eugene asked, trying to force a cheerful tone into his voice. It didn't work. He just sounded squeaky.

"Rookie, don't play with me. I know all the games, I invented them," Seventh replied. "You lost Fourth and now I got a group of punk kids asking for five-hundred pounds of ecstasy."

"Shit," Eugene replied, making Bob and Eugene freeze in their tracks.

"You know the rule about negotiations. Clear the area. We are going in," Seventh told Eugene.

"Seventh no, wait. Please don't do it," Eugene almost screamed into the phone.

"Don't do what?" Shorty asked, but Eugene ignored him.

"I got Death's team working with me. Give me some time," Eugene begged Seventh.

"Rookie, this is serious," Seventh replied.

"You need to give us more time, please." Sweat poured down Eugene's brow.

"The kidnappers want their ransom by tomorrow at nine p.m. I'm giving you until seven. Don't let me down," Seventh told Eugene and disconnected.

"We are so dead," Eugene told Bob and Shorty, feeling his face heating up.

"What do you mean by *we*?" Shorty asked Eugene. "I don't like the word we, especially when it comes to dying," Shorty told Bob.

"Eugene, what's going on?" Bob asked him in a soft voice.

Eugene felt like a scared child, pulling on his button nonstop as he stared at the ground. "Our werewolves called the lab asking for a ransom of five-hundred pounds of ecstasy," Eugene told them.

"What? Who do they think they are?" Shorty asked, almost choking on his spit. "Besides, they don't deserve to get paid for accidentally finding someone. That's cheating. They didn't do anything." Shorty's hands went to his hips as he tapped his foot furiously against the ground.

"Was Seventh able to trace the call?" Bob asked Eugene.

"Of course not. Not everyone has a mini-Bart on staff. No luck there," Eugene told him as he started pacing again. "We have another problem." Eugene stopped pacing and dropped his head in resignation.

"I don't like the sound of your voice," Shorty told Eugene.

"What else is going on?" Bob asked.

"We have a no negotiation clause," Eugene said.

"So what? We do too. Even the US government has one. What's the big deal?" Bob asked, frowning.

"Does your clause involve gassing the entire town and killing everyone within a ten-mile radius of the potential target?" Eugene asked, waving his hands in the air like a madman.

"Holy Shit! You guys are nuts," Shorty yelled. "Would you kill your own guy to avoid negotiations?"

"That's the catch, Shorty. The only person that would survive would be their guy, since they are immune to poisons, chemicals, and even plagues," Bob explained. "Insane and vicious."

"E, I don't want to die. I'm too talented to die. Shit, I'm too handsome to die," Shorty rambled.

"Yeah Shorty, you are too modest to die," Bob told him sarcastically. "I do agree with Shorty, though. Dying was not on my list of things to do this week. Not to mention, I'm sure Constantine would not appreciate Pestilence's plans." Bob glanced at Eugene, then turned to watch Shorty, who was now pacing instead of Eugene.

"Good news. Seventh is giving us twenty-four hours to get Fourth back before they gas the place," Eugene said, squeezing his hands over and over.

"Why are all of our deadlines impossible to meet?" Shorty asked from behind Bob, trying to pace and talk at the same time.

"Pressure makes diamonds," Bob told Shorty.

"Right, but it also busts pipes. I think we are in the busting department today," Shorty replied, crossing his arms.

"Can we do it?" Eugene asked softly.

"We don't have a choice. Dying is not an option. Besides, I doubt we can evacuate the whole town by telling them that Pestilence is going to kill them," Bob told Eugene.

"We could put it on TxkToday," Shorty told him. "Their Facebook page has tons of followers." Bob and Eugene both raised their eyebrows at Shorty. "Don't judge. I like their page."

"If we tell anyone, the Mistress will kill us first," Eugene tried to explain.

"In that case, it sounds like we got work to do," Bob told them. "Shorty, you need to get the underground mobilized now."

"Sounds like a plan," Shorty told Bob and ran to his truck.

"Eugene, we need to get the hearse back to Reapers and find your werewolves. We also need to figure out what they plan to do with the drugs they already have," Bob told Eugene.

"Hopefully snort it, then we won't have to worry about them," Eugene told him, feeling mischievous.

"Now Eugene, it isn't nice to wish harm on others." Bob shook his head.

"You do remember I work for Pestilence. We wish harm on everyone," Eugene said.

"True. I keep forgetting that," Bob agreed. "Follow me in the hearse. I'll give an update to the boss from the truck."

Bob went over to Storm and Eugene jumped in the hearse. Luckily for Eugene, they always kept a spare key at the bottom of the center console. After having the hearse stolen, Eugene realized that might not be the best plan for security.

After a deep breath or two, Eugene followed Bob out of the parking lot.

CHAPTER 4

Reapers had the same security system for vehicles in the back as it did for pedestrians in the front. Eugene parked the hearse behind Reapers, then jumped in Storm with Bob to get inside. After clearing all the securities, they rushed upstairs to the loft.

When they entered the loft, Bartholomew sat at his computer station like usual. On the other hand, Constantine paced the length of the kitchen island, and Eugene had to do a double take. Constantine looked way bigger than normal.

"Genocides is Pestilence's policy on ransoms and blackmail. Are you kidding me?" Constantine hissed at Eugene. "Do I want to know how many times she has done this?" He grew larger with every word, which made fear penetrate Eugene's gut. He didn't want to go near that angry cat.

"Probably not," Eugene answered in a soft voice.

"Boss, it's not Eugene's fault," Bob said to Constantine.

"Technically it is. He lost the stupid drugs." Constantine stopped pacing. "Explain yourself. How did those sad excuses for wolves find you anyway? How often do you go to the field?" Constantine somehow stared down at Eugene, and he had no idea how the cat did it.

"I stop by the field every Monday, Wednesday, and Friday at seven a.m. on my way to the club. Then I stop again on my way back to the lab," Eugene confessed.

"Please tell me you take a different route each time?" Bob asked.

"Am I supposed to?" Eugene asked, looking at Bob.

"Of course you are, silly," Constantine answered, covering his eyes with his paw. "They pretty much followed you and found your weak spot. You might as well have just handed them the drugs yourself because that's how easy you made it. Bob, you need to teach this child some combat skills or he might get himself killed."

He went back to pacing, but this time he shook his head while he did.

"What are we going to do?" Eugene did not want to spend the next year locked away in the lab. Also, he'd grown rather fond of Texarkana, so he really didn't want to see it wiped off the map.

"First, we need to find your new fans and get your buddy back," Constantine told him.

Before Eugene could ask any more questions, Eric burst through the door. Eric was Reapers martial arts trainer, witch on call, and town cop. He was also tall, good looking, and smooth. It impressed Eugene how secure he always appeared.

"Oh no, I was hoping it was all a coincidence," Eric said in greeting.

"This can't be good," Constantine said as he looked Eric up and down.

"We got three kids in the ER. Drug overdose," Eric told them. "One managed to say he got a new packet of the Mistress Special. I only know one person capable of creating high dosage drugs that calls herself the Mistress," he finished, and his eyes fell on Eugene.

"You sell the stuff as well?" Constantine asked, yelling at Eugene.

Eugene threw his hands out in front of him and waved them back and forth. "No, no. It isn't like that. We only sell at the club and it's closed this early in the morning." When he finished, he let his arms fall to his side as he looked at the floor. It didn't matter what he said. He'd never be able to talk his way out of this one.

"Do I want to know what club you are talking about?" Eric asked.

"Not at all. I would hate to accessorize you with compromising info. Just know it wasn't us," Eugene told Eric.

"Not exactly, at least," Bob jumped in.

"What Bob is trying to say is this: Pestilence and her team did not sell those drugs to those kids. However, the drugs do belong to her," Constantine clarified for Eric.

"If you guys are not selling them, who is?" Eric's cop-mode interrogation skills were coming out as he questioned Eugene.

"A gang of werewolves stole a hundred pounds from me this morning," Eugene said, dropping his head.

"By the stars," Eric said. "The kid said he took less than a teaspoon and that thing almost killed him. We are going to have bodies piling high if we don't find them." He moaned, then started pacing.

There was way too much pacing going on today. Eugene didn't like it one bit.

"Oh, it gets worse. If we don't find them in the next twenty-four hours, Pestilence's team will kill the whole town," Constantine told Eric.

"Over the drugs? She didn't try that with the zombie apocalypse." Eric's eyes flicked from Bob to Eugene and finally landed on Constantine.

"They have Fourth and they are asking for a ransom," Eugene added, taking a seat at the dining table. He was getting the Monday morning blues and his head hurt.

"Please tell me you have a plan." Eric focused on Constantine. "Is Isis already looking for the gang?"

"Isis is in Jefferson working on her own mission. We are not going to tell her about this small incident," Constantine told Eric.

"Small incident? They are threatening to wipe out the city." Eric's voice got louder with each word he spoke.

"Eric, we are not telling Isis. Got it?" Constantine posed his last words as a question, but it wasn't a question that had any other answer than "yes."

"Fine," Eric replied. It made Eugene feel better to see the fabulous Eric looking flustered. He always envied how Isis acted around him.

"Bartholomew, please tell me you found something," Constantine shouted in the direction of Bartholomew.

"Sorry Constantine, I'm still looking," Bartholomew yelled, headphones on his head and his eyes on the computer screen.

"We are in trouble if Bart can't even look in our direction when he speaks," Eugene told them.

"He is trying to cross reference every surveillance camera the city has for this potential gang," Constantine explained.

"Information I really did not want to know," Eric told him. "In the meantime, what can I do? I really don't need a bunch of dead kids in Texarkana."

"That's a really good point. If Death finds out, we are all toast," Constantine told them. "Eugene, we need an antidote for your super-drug." He left no room for argument.

"Not again," Eugene whined. "You know our policy on cures.

We don't do them." He threw his hands in the air.

"Do you want Death tracking down Pestilence because of your little drug issue?" Constantine asked.

"That would be awful. The Mistress would skin me alive," Eugene said, his tone defeated.

"I have a feeling she actually would do that, too," Bob told him.

"Fine, but I'm going to need supplies. Lots and lots of supplies," Eugene said, pouting. He was the only one of Pestilence's Interns that ever had to make cures for his experiments, which gave him a horrible track record.

"Just make up a list and I got you," Bob told him.

"You will probably need to go to the lab to get most of the stuff," Eugene told him, biting his lips.

Before Bob could reply, Shorty ran through the door.

"We really need a better security system. Too many people just keep bashing in," Constantine told Bob.

"Boss, I think you gave them access," Bob told him.

"It must have been a lapse in my thinking. I was probably suffering from a food coma or something," Constantine said with an evil smirk on his face.

"Hey Eric, what's up?" Shorty greeted Eric.

"Looking good, Shorty," Eric replied.

"Been working out." Shorty flexed his muscles. The words he'd spoken had Eugene doing a double take, but nothing had changed. Shorty looked as scrawny as ever.

"Glad we are all acquainted with each other. Now, maybe we can get back to business," Constantine told the group. "Shorty, this better be good."

"Sorry boss, got distracted," Shorty apologized.

"And people have the audacity to make fun of cats for paying attention to shiny objects. The nerve," Constantine said in a mocking tone. "Spill it, we are losing time. What did you find out so fast?"

"That's the problem, Boss Man. Nobody knows anything," Shorty said.

"What do you mean?" Bob asked.

"I texted all my top people and nobody has seen any of that gang. It's like they disappeared from the earth." Shorty shrugged in resignation.

"How is that possible? You have eyes and ears everywhere," Eugene said.

"That's the point. After they left the Electric Cowboy, none of my people have been able to find them. We have no idea where they go, but they are definitely not in town," Shorty said, shaking his head.

"Please tell me we are not looking for Los Lobos?" Eric asked.

"You know them?" Bob asked.

"They are the only werewolf gang in town," Eric answered.

"We also know they won't be getting a prize for creativity," Constantine said.

"What do you mean by that, Boss?" Shorty asked, scratching his head.

"Because *Los Lobos* means *The Wolves* in Spanish," Eugene answered. "Eric, what do you know about them?" he added, trying to get everyone back to business.

"Besides being dangerous, highly trained, and heavily weapon? Their recruitment strategies are vicious, but they have a big following," Eric said in a flat tone.

"How come I'm the only one scared to death that we are dealing with werewolves?" Eugene asked.

"You are not the only one, E," Shorty told Eugene.

"That fear will keep you alive. Don't lose it," Constantine told both Shorty and Eugene. "Bartholomew, cross reference gang Los Lobos with anything in your database."

"That actually helps, thanks," Bartholomew yelled back.

"Wouldn't it be easier if we just make him take the headphones off so he can hear us?" Eric asked Constantine as he ran his fingers through his hair.

"Maybe, but he is the only one working here. The headphones cancel the noise and help him focus," Constantine told Eric. "Speaking of work, sounds like the rest of you need to get busy." Somehow he managed to stare at everyone all at once. Eugene had no idea how he did it, but he wished he had that kind of power.

"I'll check the police database for anything suspicious on Los Lobos," Eric told them right before he headed out the door.

"Shorty, we need you to mobilize the underground and warn them about the new drug on the streets. It's deadly and doesn't take much to kill," Bob told him.

"We might also need their help," Constantine told both men. "Eugene will be working on an antidote. We are going to need able bodies ready to help those overdosing." His gaze fell on Eugene.

"That's a great idea, Boss," Bob told Constantine. "Eugene, whenever you are ready with the list, I'll take off," Bob told Eugene as he pointed towards the door.

"I got a better plan. I'll text the list to Seventh. That way he will have everything ready when you get there," Eugene told Bob as he pulled his phone out. "Besides, I don't have a clue if he told anyone else. I don't need Fifth calling the Mistress and turning us in." His fingers were typing at the same time he was speaking, which made it a little difficult for him.

"It's about time you started acting like our mad-scientist." Constantine sounded proud, then turned his attention to Bob and Shorty. "Well, you two better get going now."

Both of them ran out the door.

"Do you need my help up here?" Eugene asked Constantine.

"Nope, Bartholomew and I got it covered," Constantine answered.

"In that case, I'm going to get the lab ready. We are going to need a lot of antidote," Eugene told Constantine, and then he headed out the door.

Constantine watched Eugene leave the room. The loft was finally quiet. The only sound was from Bartholomew typing at his control station.

"That boy is going to be the death of me, and he is not even my Intern," Constantine said to himself as he started grooming his face.

CHAPTER 5

It had taken Eugene almost five hours to get enough antidote ready to cover the amount of drugs the werewolves were carrying. He was exhausted, and he could only imagine how tired Bob was. Bob had done at least five trips to the lab in Hope to pick up the supplies Eugene needed. At this point, he regretted not telling Isis. She always made a great assistant when he needed one. Now they just had to deliver the vaccine to all of Shorty's people, which posed a bit of a problem. The underground did not have a centralized location, so they were going to have to drive all over Texarkana to drop it off.

Bob and Shorty decided it would be faster to start making deliveries Downtown. Texarkana and the surrounding cities might feel like small towns, but in fact they covered a very large terrain. Matching their location with the time Shorty's people were on duty was vital. The team needed to match their locations with the times Shorty's people were on duty. Eugene was in charge of demonstrating how to administer the antidote and he developed a modified EpiPen for the occasion. It was the fastest and cleanest way to carry it around. Not to mention, one person could carry ten pens without attracting too much attention. They still didn't want to create a panic in the city, unless people started dying.

It took the team over two hours driving around to find most of the informants and the active members of Shorty's crew. Eugene was amazed that Shorty had people covering the entire town.

"Last stop is Beverly's Park," Bob told Eugene.

"Where is that at?" Eugene asked as they were driving back from Liberty-Eylau.

"Right next to Big Jakes," Bob told him.

"Why didn't we start there? We have passed that place at least three times." Eugene couldn't figure out the actual distribution plan, especially since he was sure they had been driving in circles for hours.

"Unfortunately, the park crew doesn't start work until five. Hence the reason we are here now," Bob told him with a smile. "Besides the food I gave you, have you had anything to eat?" He looked at Eugene like a concern dad.

Eugene shrugged. "I was a little busy."

"You and Isis are so much alike. You run around nonstop and then are shocked when you're exhausted and moody," Bob told Eugene. "It's called being malnourished. We are stopping by Big Jakes when we are done." His tone left no room for arguments.

"Okay," Eugene replied as his stomach grumbled at the mention of food, which in his book made his stomach a traitor.

"I think your stomach agrees with me," Bob told Eugene with a smirk.

"Those sounds could be deceiving," Eugene said, but his stomach chose that moment to growl so loud he was sure there was no way Bob hadn't heard it.

Darn traitorous stomach, he thought.

Bob pulled into the park's main entrance and followed the path to the back. Shorty was right on their heels the whole way, but Eugene kind of wondered if Bob had taken the lead so Shorty would have to slow down. That way, no pedestrians would be scared away.

Bob parked next to a picnic bench where two young ladies sat. With their purple and blue hair, their ripped clothes, and the amount of make-up plastered on their face, one might confuse them for teenagers.

With a shake of his head, Eugene followed Bob out of the truck and grabbed his bag of EpiPens.

"Good afternoon ladies," Bob said.

"Hi, Big-Bob," the one with purple hair said.

"What's the huge emergency?" the blue-haired lady asked.

Eugene realized the ladies were at least mid-twenties and in great shape. Both of them looked like they would easily win a fight. . Any fight, for that matter.

"Melissa. Natalie. Meet Eugene. He is our resident scientist," Bob said to the ladies. Melissa had the purple hair, and Natalie the blue. "These ladies are our residence martial arts trainers and the toughest members of the underground."

Eugene nodded. He could believe that.

"Thanks, Big-Bob," Melissa replied, her chest puffing out with pride. Her sweet smile lit up her beautiful brown eyes.

"We have to be. We work the truck stops and sleazy motels," Natalie told Eugene in a serious tone. She had to be the leader of the two. She'd barely let out a smile, and when she looked Eugene up and down, it made him feel like some kind of lowly animal.

"What's your target?" Eugene asked. He had learned each team had a group they watched or assisted.

"We try to help the girls that have lost their way," Melissa replied.

Eugene was impressed. If these two women were in charge of helping the street walkers, that meant they dealt with a lot of angry customers.

"That is amazing. I don't know how you do it," Eugene said, and he meant every word.

Natalie smiled. "Some girls are forced into that life, and others feel they have no choice."

"They are like the Underground Railroad. Moving girls from one city to the other to keep them safe," Shorty jumped in. "Huge mission." Shorty saluted the ladies and Eugene bowed his head to them.

"Thanks. But I'm sure you are not here to sing our praises today." Natalie was back to business.

"We got serious problems, ladies," Bob said. "A deadly drug is being sold. We need your help to warn people." He pointed to Eugene.

"We have an antidote to slow the reaction if you find somebody overdosing," Eugene told the ladies as he pulled his demonstration pen out. "They will still need to be taken to the hospital, but this will give them time to get there. It's pretty simple to use. Pull the cap off and stab them in the leg. Press the top button and done." He had done the same demonstration so many times that day, he could do it with his eyes closed. Instead, he faced forward and finished showing them what to do, then he passed out pens.

"We heard about a major drug deal going on this evening," Melissa told them.

"Where?" Bob asked.

"We didn't ask." Natalie shrugged. "Anytime you start asking questions, people get suspicious and avoid you," she explained as she put some pens in her pockets.

"Makes sense, but start warning people," Bob told them. "This is one deal they will die for." Bob was serious, but Eugene giggled at the phrase.

"Will do," both ladies replied, then they took off.

"I'm out. Going to start checking on people," Shorty announced.

"Shorty, be careful," Bob told him. "We are not dealing with regular people." His worried gaze scanned the park.

"Bob, we haven't been dealing with regular people in years. We just know what they are now," Shorty replied, giving Bob a fist-bump. "Keep your head up, E. We got this." He gave Eugene a fist bump as well, then ran back to his truck.

"Why don't I feel as confident as Shorty?" Eugene asked.

"Because you are young and haven't seen as much crap as he has," Bob replied with a smile. "Let's go and get you food. It will help you focus better." He headed back towards his truck and Eugene followed.

Fortunately for Eugene, Big Jakes was located right next to the entrance to Beverly Park. Bob made a left before leaving the driveway and parked in front of the restaurant. Isis was addicted to the BBQ joint, which blew Eugene's mind since Isis didn't eat meat. She just went crazy for chilly fries and potato salad.

Eugene was so hungry that he entered the establishment almost in a trance. The place was pretty empty. The lunch crowd was long gone, and the dinner crowd had not arrived yet. It gave the place a quiet, cozy setting.

After he ordered a plate of brisket with baked beans and potato salad, Eugene slipped into a booth by the window. Bob placed his order, going for the pulled pork sandwich, and joined him. They both stared took in the view as they drank their sweet tea and waited for their food.

"Here is your meal, boys," a tall guy in his mid-twenties said as he slid their plates on the table.

"TJ, hey. What's going on?" Bob asked the guy.

"Saw you guys come in and wanted to say hi," TJ told them with a huge smile. "Eugene, I'm surprised to see you on a Monday." Everyone knew Eugene's schedule, and he only came to Big Jakes on Friday nights with the Reaper crew.

"Long, crazy story, but right now you are my favorite person in town. I'm starving," Eugene admitted. TJ grinned as Eugene placed a large piece of brisket in his mouth and devoured it.

"Hey TJ, what do you know about Los Lobos?" Bob asked, taking a small bite of his sandwich.

"That's a rough group. They are dangerous and volatile. If possible, I recommend staying away from them." TJ lowered his voice and looked over his shoulder, like he expected them to be behind him.

"I wish, but they have something we need," Bob told him.

"And they have my friend," Eugene mumbled between mouthfuls.

"In that case, you can probably find them on a Monday night at the Cave," TJ told them.

"The Cave?" asked Bob, his gaze springing from TJ to Eugene.

"Do you know another place run by the devil?" TJ questioned Bob.

"Oh yeah, that's the one," Eugene said.

"You look like such a wholesome, American guy, but I have a feeling there is so much more we don't know about you. You are always full of info," Bob told TJ, giving him a careful look.

Eugene stopped eating and stared at TJ as well. Bob was right, there was something different about him. Almost inhuman.

"Hey, people just talk to me." TJ shrugged, then he padded Bob in the shoulder before heading back to the kitchen.

"There is something different about him that I haven't noticed before," Eugene told Bob.

"I always had that feeling when it came to TJ, but we are all entitled to our secrets," Bob told Eugene. "Unfortunately, if TJ is right, you know what that means?" He eyed Eugene as he pulled his phone from his pocket.

"I have never been to the Cave without Isis. I'm not ready," Eugene mumbled to Bob.

"Hey Boss, we got a problem," Bob said, ignoring Eugene. Eugene couldn't hear the other side of the conversation, but he had a feeling Bob was talking to Constantine. "No luck on the gang. But we have a lead that they might be at the Cave tonight. What should we do?"

Bob was quiet for just a few minutes as he nodded his head. The anticipation was killing Eugene, but he waited. Last thing he needed was Constantine mad at him for interrupting.

"Got it," Bob replied and disconnected to the call.

"Just tell me. What did he say?" Eugene asked Bob, trying to rush him.

"Just like I feared, you are going to the Cave," Bob told Eugene, a frown on his face. Which made sense. Bob hated the devil, and refused to set foot inside his establishment. Which meant it would be Eugene going in. "The theme tonight is the seventies. We need to get you some clothes, so we better hurry."

Both of them finished their meals in record time, then they went shopping.

CHAPTER 6

Jake, or Jacob, the deceiver commonly known as the devil, ran the hottest club in the world. The Cave was invitation only, and you could only enter if you knew where the door would be. According to Isis and Constantine, doors appeared all over the world, in many different cities. Unfortunately, the doors changed locations each day, even in the same city. Jake enjoyed making things complicated for people.

Last time Eugene went to the Cave with Isis, the door was located near the entrance to the federal jail. Eugene had freaked, not wanting to be arrested for breaking into a clandestine club. For that occasion, Isis used her magical gifts from Death to keep people away, making their entrance easy and jail free. She was like the walking pied piper, except hotter.

"We are in luck; the entrance is on the side of Books-A-Million," Bob told Eugene.

Eugene wasn't sure if he agreed with Bob's definition of luck. Not only did he have to walk outside wearing a white John Travolta suit from *Saturday Night Fever,* he had to do it in July in Texarkana. Plus, he was a black man in an all-white suit walking around a book store. He looked shady.

At this rate, Eric *was* going to have to bail him out of jail.

"Why are people heading to Books-A-Million on a Monday night?" Eugene asked Bob.

Bob pulled the truck into the parking lot. "Because it's July in Texarkana and kids are off school," he said as he found a parking space near the entrance.

"I'm going to stick out," Eugene said, pointing to the crowd of teenagers hanging outside.

"Of course you are, but at least you'll look fly doing it," Bob replied.

Funnily enough, Eugene didn't feel "fly" at all.

"Fine, I'm doing this. You are planning to wait here, right?" Eugene asked before stepping out of the truck.

"Eugene, go. I'll be right here. Just hurry up," Bob said as he waved him away.

They had no other choice, so Eugene closed the door of the truck with a big sigh. He fixed his hair one more time and checked his jacket. He *did* look good. Now, he just needed to make sure he didn't get killed. He channeled his inner Travolta and made his way towards the side of the building with lots of swagger. Like usual, as he got closer to the door, bouncers appeared. He had no idea how they did it, but they always appeared at the last possible moment.

Eugene knew one of the guys, or at least he thought he did. His name was Adam, but his hair color was different than the last time Eugene had seen him. He'd been blond then, and today jet black. Adam, like every person who worked at the Cave, was disgustingly handsome. The other guy also looked like a model, with brown hair that had some strange highlights. Eugene was sure the ladies loved that stuff, but it made every man extremely self-conscious.

"Eugene. My man. Looking hot," Adam told him, giving him a fist-bump. Eugene was grateful he didn't get a hug.

"What's up Adam? I'm here to see your boss. Constantine sent me," Eugene told Adam. He didn't have the same relationship Isis had with this crew, which made it harder for him. In fact, he had started fixing his jacket the moment he'd stepped inside.

"His highness is right inside," Adam replied.

"Thanks Adam, I know the drill," Eugene told Adam as he walked through the magical curtains that led down to the club.

"Do you think he knows he only had to dress up today?" the brunette asked Adam after Eugene had entered the club.

"I doubt it. Which means this could be one hell of a show. Watch the door, I'm heading inside," Adam replied and followed Eugene.

Eugene didn't waste any time starting his dance routine after descending the magical stairs and clearing the second set of curtains. On his previous visit, the theme had been Latin music. Isis and he had to dance their way through the floor to get to the devil without getting killed. Latin music was his favorite, but he knew every move from the movie Saturday Night Fever, which meant Eugene was more than prepared for tonight.

The club looked exactly like a place you would find back in the seventies, including the people smoking. Eugene found Jake leaning on a tall table on the opposite side of the dance floor. Jake, like the rest of his men, was extremely handsome with blond hair. He looked like a young Brad Pitt.

Eugene adjusted his shirt, loosened the button on his jacket, and stepped on the dance floor.

While most people were nervous in clubs, Eugene was the opposite. He was a different person on the dance floor. His confidence increased, his rhythm was impeccable, and his moves made people turn and stare. This night was no different. He was a dancing king and he knew it. He had all of Travolta's moves memorized, starting with his *Grease* days and including *Pulp Fiction*. Eugene was on fire. At one point, he was even convinced one of the ladies on the dance floor was coming to attack him. Eugene took her by the hand, gave her a fast spin followed by a dip and sent her on her way. He made his way across the floor, ending with a split and bouncing up in a flash. The crowd went wild.

"Eugene, like usual, your dancing skills are impressive," Jake told Eugene, saluting him with his glass.

"Jake, sir. I'm here on business," Eugene told the devil as he wiped the sweat from his face with his handkerchief. He had worked a lot harder than he'd expected on that little number.

"Of course. What do you need?" Jake asked Eugene as he sipped his drink without a care in the world.

"We are looking for a gang of werewolves that patron your place. They called themselves Los Lobos," Eugene told Jake, leaning in to whisper so he sounded more serious.

"What would I get for the information?" Jake asked him.

"What do you mean? I just danced my way over here for it," Eugene told him, stomping at the floor.

"Sorry my boy, dancing doesn't cover talking to me tonight. What you are asking is betraying the trust of my clients," Jake told Eugene with a wicked smile. "You need to make it worth my time."

"Isis told me I can't give you my soul. Not to mention, I'm pretty sure the Mistress already has claims on it," Eugene confessed to Jake.

"I don't doubt that," Jake concurred. "I'm sure we can come up with another arrangement." As he twirled the straw in his drink, Jake smiled and looked more dangerous than he ever had before.

Eugene swallowed. Hard. "What do you have in mind?"

"I need three cases of tear gas for this weekend," Jake told him.

"What for? You run a club," Eugene asked, his gaze roaming said *club*.

"I'm the devil. I have my hands in many things," Jake told him. "If you must know, I'm sponsoring a teacher's strike in the Caribbean and it's going to be a wild one." When he finished, he rubbed his hands together, completing his diabolical look perfectly.

There was no point in arguing. Eugene knew he'd never beat the devil at his own game. "Fine, I'll get you three cases. Now, what do you know?"

"They are right behind you. Three tables down from us," Jake told Eugene, pointing in the direction he'd just come from. Eugene turned around to find a table with three tall guys and one tough-looking chick.

"What? You are freaking kidding me. I just paid you for that?" Anger fueled Eugene as he leaned across the table and grabbed the devil by his shirt, considering how he could strangle him.

"It is not my fault you didn't pay attention to your surroundings," Jake answered. "I want my crates this Friday."

"Fine," Eugene muttered in an angry tone. The group looked like they were getting ready to leave, so Eugene readied himself to follow, but Jake stopped him.

"Where do you think you are going?" Jake asked Eugene as he pulled him back.

"They are leaving, so I'm going after them," Eugene answered, trying to jerk away from Jake.

"How far do you think you will get before they see you? Look at your clothes," Jake pointed at Eugene's white suit as he spoke.

"What do you want me to do? Walk around naked?" Eugene eyed his suit.

"For a crate of swine flu, I can hook you up with another fabulous outfit," Jake told Eugene with a wink.

"How come this doesn't happen to Isis?" Eugene asked.

"She comes prepared," Jake admitted. "Better decide fast; your little pups are leaving." He smirked at his own joke.

Eugene threw his hands in the air. "Fine, I'll bring that too. Now hurry." This was the last time he'd ever be making a deal with the devil.

Jake snapped his fingers and Eugene's white suit was gone. In its place was a fabulous black hoodie, with black cargo pants, and a black cap. Eugene looked down at himself.

"Are you kidding me? What is this, racial profiling?" Eugene told Jake in a high-pitched tone.

"You got jokes today, Eugene. It's called camouflage. You are tracking them at night. I even covered your scent," Jake told Eugene, smiling.

"You can do that?" Eugene glared at Jake.

"Yes I can. You know why? Because I'm the devil. You can sit here and admire me all night but your group is heading out the door." Jake pointed behind Eugene.

"Oh damn," Eugene told Jake and ran after the werewolves.

"There is something seriously wrong with that child," Adam told Jake as he walked up next to him.

"He works for Pestilence, definitely not his fault. But he is one great dresser," Jake told Adam as he snapped his fingers. Jake was wearing a replica of Eugene's white suit. He brushed his hands down the smooth fabric and smiled at Adam.

"Looking good, your highness," Adam told Jake as he walked around his boss. "By the way, the elven Princess and Vampire heir are waiting for you." Adam pointed across the dance floor as he came to a stop in front of his boss.

"I love those two," Jake told Adam with a smile. "I'm ready to party." He crossed the floor, doing his own dance moves and making the crowd cheer.

CHAPTER 7

E ugene ran to the truck and jumped inside. Bob looked him up and down, rubbing his temples.

"The last four people who left the club were our werewolves. Did you see them?" Eugene asked Bob as he struggled to buckle his seatbelt. Bob took off before Eugene was finished.

"Way ahead of you. I had Bartholomew run all the license plates for every car in the parking lot and cross reference with our guys. He got them. They are driving a red Toyota pickup," Bob told Eugene as he headed out of the parking lot of Books-A-Million. "Bartholomew is tracking them now." He took a right turn on the service road and headed towards Summerhill Road.

"That's impressive," Eugene told Bob. Bob and Bartholomew had been a lot more productive than he had been inside the club.

"I had to keep myself busy while I waited for you," Bob told him, not making eye contact.

"Bob, they are entering Spring Lake." Bartholomew's voice came through the speaker system.

"Not that park again," Eugene told them. "I think that place is haunted."

"Not anymore," Bartholomew replied. "Isis collected all the wandering souls last May. It's ghost free." There was pride in Bartholomew's tone when he spoke of Isis, and it made Eugene wish someone would speak of him that way one day.

"In that case, the place is cursed," Eugene added.

"That is a good possibility," Bob told him.

"Yeah, we don't deal in curses, just souls," Bartholomew told him. "Okay Bob, they parked right in front of the baseball fields," he said, changing the subject back to the matter at hand.

"Anything going on in the area?" Bob asked Bartholomew.

"I'm checking now," Bartholomew told Bob. "Oh no, Bob. You

better hurry. The Texarkana Twins are playing a home game tonight. It's going to be packed." His voice cracked.

"Told you. Cursed," Eugene told Bob.

"Maybe. Hold on now," Bob told Eugene as he took the right to enter the park a little too fast. "Eugene, we have EpiPens with us, right?" Bob asked as he found a parking space.

"Over two hundred," Eugene replied, reaching for his bag in the back seat.

"Fill your pockets. I have a feeling we are going to need them," Bob told Eugene. "Bartholomew, you might want to give Eric a heads up. This could be bad."

"Will do. Be careful over there," Bartholomew told them as he disconnected the call.

"Are you ready?" Eugene asked Bob.

"I am, but you might want to change your shirt. You look suspicious with a hoodie in July." Bob pointed at the back seat.

"I knew it. Jake set me up," Eugene told Bob as he grabbed a t-shirt from the back seat. "Do you always carry extra clothes with you?" he asked as he pulled on a gray t-shirt.

"Isis is accident prone, which means you always have extra clothes when she is around," Bob told Eugene.

Eugene couldn't agree more. Isis had a way of always getting dirty or wet.

After Eugene changed his top, he stuffed his pockets with EpiPens. He was hoping they wouldn't need them all, but he had a feeling they would.

Bob climbed out of the truck and Eugene followed. They inched towards the field where The Twins were playing. Bob paid for tickets and they walked in.

"Should we split up?" Eugene asked.

"Won't be necessary," Bob told him. "They are over there by the party deck near the bouncy house." Eugene followed Bob's gaze and found two of the werewolves from the club talking to a couple of the staff from the event.

"Where is the girl and the other guy? There were four of them," Eugene asked, scanning the area.

"That's a good question. I don't—"

A woman's scream cut Bob short.

"Oh God!" another lady screamed. "He is dying."

"Let's go," Bob and Eugene ran in the direction of the screams.

As soon as they were around the bleachers, Eugene spotted two teenagers on the ground, seizing and foaming at the mouth. People screamed around them, their wide eyes searching for anyone who could help. Panic set the tone in the arena.

"What's going on?" screamed one of the coaches from the field. "Hey, that's my son." The coach ran towards them.

"Everyone relax. We are EMTs, let us through," Eugene announced, and the crowd cleared for them. They rushed to the boys just as their convulsions intensified.

"Eugene, is this supposed to look like this?" Bob asked Eugene.

"Yes, at least for this drug. You know the drill. Hurry, they don't have much time," Eugene told Bob. Almost in unison, they pulled EpiPens out and stabbed the boys in the leg. Within seconds, the boys stopped shaking and foaming.

"Help! Over here," a male voice yelled from across the other set of bleachers. Bob stood up to find more teenagers dropping.

"Eugene, we need to hurry. There are casualties everywhere," Bob told Eugene as he ran to the other side.

"Keep an eye on them and call an ambulance. They need to be taken to a hospital now," Eugene told one of the ladies and the coach.

"Thank you so much," the lady told him.

"What happened to him?" the coach asked.

"Looks like a horrible allergic reaction to something. Don't leave him alone," Eugene told the coach. He didn't want to go into a lengthy explanation about the drugs.

"But he is not allergic to anything," the coach shouted.

"Sorry, Sir. I don't know what else to tell you. I have to go." Eugene took off before the coach could reply.

Bob was having a hard time keeping up with all the casualties, so Eugene ran over and started injecting every kid he found. Some were overdosing faster than others. If only he had more time to analyze their reactions to the drug, but people were dropping left and right, which left only enough time to find them and give them the antidote.

"How are they passing this out?" Eugene asked Bob after the tenth kid.

"Caramel," Bob replied back. "I found several wrappers around some of the kids. They are selling them as candy, literally." He moved to the next one.

"We need to ban the sale of food items in this city. People are too trusting here," Eugene told Bob, thinking of his last incident.

"Sure, start a petition after we fix this mess," Bob told him, jumping to another girl who was foaming on the ground.

"Where are they?" Eugene asked as he moved to another kid.

"They are long gone. Saw them leaving once the bodies started falling," Bob told Eugene. "There, that's the last one." Bob stood over his last patient and took inventory. There were over twenty kids on the ground.

"What is going on?" The empire rushed over to them, his words so loud Eugene had to stop himself from covering his ears with his hands.

"We think the candy is contaminated. Can you make an announcement for people not to eat it?" Eugene told the empire.

"Of course. On my way." The empire ran to the nearest microphone and made the announcement.

"Holy crap, what happened?" Eric asked Eugene and Bob as he came up beside them.

"Sorry Eric, my thighs are cramping," Eugene told Eric as he sat on the ground next to his last patient.

"Not you Eugene. I was referring to all the people around you." Eric pointed at all the comatose kids everywhere.

"Oh them, my bad," Eugene replied as he got off the ground.

"Our favorite gang of wolves did this in less than ten minutes," Bob told him, wiping his hands on his handkerchief.

"How is that possible?" Eric asked him. "These are kids. I'm sure most of them were not using drugs before today." He looked at the kids in disbelief.

"That's the problem. They are lacing candy with the drugs," Eugene told him.

"Not that again. Can we forbid the sale of sweets in Texarkana?" Eric asked both men.

"Thank you. I asked the same question," Eugene told Eric, sticking out his chest in his Superman pose.

"Until either one of you can figure out how to pull that off, the answer is no," Bob said, popping their bubbles.

Sirens blared in the distance. "It's about time. They need a hospital soon," Eugene told them.

Bob's phone rang, and he looked at the caller ID with a frown. "Shorty, what's going on?" he said in a form of a greeting.

"That cannot be a good call," Eugene told Eric.

"Probably not," Eric replied. "Tell me, what did you do to stop them from overdosing?" he asked Eugene.

"Hit them with a dose of the antidote," Eugene told Eric, holding up an EpiPen.

"Do you have any more?" Eric asked.

"We got tons in the truck," Eugene told him.

"Eugene, we have to go," Bob told him. "Shorty has another outbreak at the student center at Texas A&M," Bob told them. Eugene and Eric followed him out, but Bob stopped and turned to Eric. "You should probably stay here and explain what happened."

"I have become the messenger of death. Every time something bad happens, I'm the one explaining it," Eric told Bob. He wasn't whining about it, just stating a fact. "Let's hope I don't get fired because people start thinking I'm the one doing these awful things." Eric shook his head.

"Just tell them you have really good connections," Eugene told Eric, more than meaning his words.

"That's a good idea, and you aren't technically lying," Bob agreed with Eugene.

"At this rate, I need to tell my captain something," Eric told them.

"Here." Eugene passed Eric about twenty EpiPens. "This should hold you over for a while. I hope." Eugene sighed as he glanced at the field.

Eugene gave Eric a quick demonstration with the EpiPen. Thankfully, he knew the technique, so Eugene didn't have to go over it too much. After only a few minutes, Eugene and Bob jumped in the truck and left Eric behind to explain everything to the cops and paramedics who were arriving by the dozen.

CHAPTER 8

On a normal Monday night, there was very little traffic in Texarkana, which made getting around easy. Today, though, it felt like it was taking forever. Bob had to drive down to the overpasses on Stateline to get to the other side of the interstate. All the one way roads were making Eugene insane. To make matters worse, Bob was driving almost as fast as Shorty, only he wasn't trying to run over every other driver on the road.

Soon enough, Bob made it down the Saint Michael Drive, then he made a right turn on Richmond and tried to drive as fast as possible to University Drive.

"What are all these people doing out?" Eugene finally asked. He couldn't help himself, they were moving so slowly.

"I'm pretty sure this is the usual crowd," Bob said.

"Why are you not worried? Eugene asked Bob.

"Eugene, in the last ten months we have been all over the country, seen the scariest ghost you can imagine, and the whole time everyone has been panicking." Bob took a quick breath before continuing. "At some point in time, you just realize that this is our life. When everything is a fire, it's no longer an emergency. It becomes standard procedure. No need to panic," he said in a straightforward tone, right as he cut off three vehicles and continued down Richmond at full speed.

"What are you trying to tell me?" Eugene asked Bob, squinting vigorously as he tried to focus on Bob.

"To relax or you are going to give yourself a heart attack," Bob told him. "It is still early and it's going to be a long night, so pace yourself." Bob made another right turn at University Drive and headed towards the A&M campus in Texarkana.

The campus had recently been renovated and new buildings were added to the complex. Eugene was amazed how collegiate the place looked, even in the middle of Texarkana.

"Shorty said they were near the student center. I'm pulling up as close as possible," Bob told Eugene, ignoring all the signs that said, "Do Not Enter."

"Aren't you afraid of getting towed?" Eugene asked Bob.

"Who's going to do it?" Bob asked. "I think everyone is a bit busy now." He pointed at the chaos in front of him. "Hope you got plenty of pens."

"Just refilled my pockets as I was helping Eric," Eugene told Bob as they both climbed out of the truck.

Eugene and Bob ran across the quad toward a large crowd of screaming college students. The school had a bonfire in the middle and the scene looked like it had come straight out of a *Friday the Thirteenth* movie. College students were collapsing left and right. Some had already started foaming at the mouth. The rest were screaming in pain.

"Shorty!" Bob shouted.

Shorty came running with three large men behind him. Their faces were pale and they looked ready to bolt.

"Big Bob, what is going on here?" Shorty asked him.

"Why are you asking us? We just got here," Eugene yelled so he could be heard over the screams.

"They are overdosing," Bob told Shorty. "Stop being a smart ass, Eugene," he added and Eugene shrugged.

"How?" one of the men behind Shorty asked. "None of these kids took any drugs."

"We have been watching them. They have been eating hot dogs and burgers," another of the three men added.

"Do we know each other?" Bob asked.

"Big Bob, these are the triplets," Shorty said. "Triplets, that's Big Bob. You know who he is. This is E, scientist extraordinaire."

Eugene couldn't help it. His chest swelled at Shorty's introduction.

Eugene scrunched his forehead. "No offense, but you guys don't look like triplets." It was true. All three men had different heights, hair colors, and nationalities.

"Maybe not by birth, but they are all named John. So triplets it is," Shorty clarified, and all three men nodded in agreement.

"Works for me," Eugene said, seeing no sense in arguing.

"We can discuss name selections later. Right now, we need to get to work," Bob told all five men. "Triplets, take the right side. Do you know how to administer the antidote?" Bob asked.

"Yes sir," all three replied in unison.

"Maybe they are triplets," Eugene whispered to Bob, who nodded in agreement.

"Good, get going," Bob said, and he hadn't even finished his statement before they took off. He turned to Shorty and Eugene. "Okay, we will take the left and we better hurry." Bob pointed, and they all took off running.

It took them longer than they expected. For every college student they administered the antidote to, another one fell over. Bob had managed to send a text to Constantine and Bartholomew for an update and to get Eric down to the school. The students were going to need medical attention soon.

An hour and a half later, with the help of the paramedics, they had all the students in stable condition. Once the situation was contained, Bob, Shorty, and Eugene started asking questions. Weirdly enough, nobody had seen anything. Also, there were no strangers passing out candy.

"We are in luck," Eric told Eugene and Bob, who were standing alone on the far side of the quad.

"What is your definition of luck?" Eugene asked Eric, examining the students being loaded into the ambulances.

"At least this was only the summer crowd and not the full student body," Eric answered.

"You have a good point," Eugene conceded.

"But how are they passing this stuff out?" Bob asked. "I checked the area and nothing looks out of the ordinary." His eyes roamed, as if he was still looking for clues.

"Excuse me." A female college student walked up to the trio. "Are you guys FBI?" she asked in a soft voice. The young lady looked like an older version of Shirley Temple. She had a small frame, probably standing less than five feet tall. She also had the cutest curls on the planet. Eugene had the desire to pet her, but he held himself back.

"Sorry, young lady, but he is the only police officer in the group," Bob told future-Shirley in the most professional voice he had.

"I saw you out there. You must work for a government agency," future-Shirley told them, not backing down.

"Oh, we work for a couple different agencies, just not the ones you know," Eugene told her, thinking of the Horsemen.

"In that case, you are here to stop this from happening again, right?" future-Shirley asked, tears filling her eyes as she glanced at the injured students.

"That's our plan," Bob told her. "Did you see what happened?"

"It was a weird," future-Shirley said, crying now. "This group of people came in, saying they were from a cooking show and they were here to do a throw down with us. They said the catch was that everyone had to use their special BBQ sauce." At her words, all three men looked at each other.

"When did the students start getting sick?" Eric asked

"Nothing happened at first," future-Shirley said. "Everyone was bragging about the food. But the more they ate, the more they wanted. Then the group started selling samples of their special sauce. Within ten minutes, the first person started having a seizure. Then all hell broke loose." Future-Shirley's tears turned to sobs.

"Why are you not sick?" Eugene asked the young lady, suspicion coating his words.

"I'm a vegetarian," future-Shirley said between sobs. "I just stayed because my best friend was trying to hook me up on a date. And now they are all dead." Future-Shirley fell to the floor and buried her head in her lap, her shoulders shaking from her sobs.

"And I thought I was dramatic," Eugene mumbled to Bob.

"At least we met someone worse," Bob replied in a teasing tone.

"Ma'am, please calm down," Eric told the young lady.

"Breathe now, before you pass out," Eugene added. "They are not dead, but your friends are going to be out for a couple a days at least. They will need to get their stomachs pumped, probably be under medical observation, and maybe have a few IV's, but other than that, they will be fine," Eugene finished with a smile, hoping to make her feel better.

Bob and Eric shook their heads.

"Dear, it's going to be okay. I recommend checking with the school officials and seeing how you can help," Bob told future-Shirley in a comforting voice.

The young lady wiped her tears and gathered herself from the floor. She gave Bob a hug, then took off running.

"How come you got the hug?" Eugene asked.

"Probably because I didn't scare her to death with facts," Bob told Eugene, shaking his head.

Eric raised his hand. "I second Bob."

"Thank you for taking his side," Eugene replied, rolling his eyes. "Now what are we going to do? I wasn't expecting our dear wolves to become so creative with their delivery system." Even to himself, Eugene sounded defeated.

"I have a fear they learned a few tricks from your dear accountant and our zombie apocalypse," Eric told Eugene.

"That thing is going to haunt me forever," Eugene said.

"Or until we have the next horrible disaster, and with our luck, it won't take long," Bob told Eugene.

"With Isis around, it's only a matter of time," Eric said. "What is that sound?" Eric and Bob looked around. The song *Smooth Criminal* was playing.

"Oh sorry, that's my phone," Eugene said, his cheeks growing a little warmer. "Hello."

"Rookie, my man, we got a problem," a man shouted over the loud music playing in the background. Eugene pulled the receiver away from his ear so he could hear and not go deaf.

"What's going on, Roy?" Eugene asked, his tone heavy with confusion.

"I have a group of punks selling E in our territory. Should we take them out?" Roy asked. Eric and Bob both moved closer and turned their ears towards the phone.

"No, Roy," Eugene almost shouted into the phone. "We need them alive. Keep an eye on them, but don't let them sell anything. Their product is contaminated. I'm on my away."

"Hurry up. This could get nasty," Roy blurted before he ended the call.

"The nerve of those punks," Eugene said, definitely shouting this time. "They are trying to out sell me in my own shop. Forget polio, I'm giving them small pox." He paced, his anger needing an outlet of some sort.

"Small pox? What are you talking about?" Eric asked Eugene.

"You don't want to know," Bob told Eric. "Let's go, Eugene. You can tell me the address to the club on the way to the truck." He patted him on the back, trying to calm Eugene down.

"If you need back up, call me," Eric told Bob.

"Will do. Could you tell Shorty and the triplets that we are out?" Bob asked Eric as he pointed at the four men assisting the paramedics.

"I got them. Good luck," Eric told Bob right before he made his way towards Shorty and the Triplets.

"Let's go, Eugene. We need to hurry," Bob told Eugene and together, they ran towards the truck.

"We really need to. The club is Downtown at the old Coliseum," Eugene told Bob

"Of course it is," Bob said and they both ran faster. Eugene thought he should probably start running every day like Isis did. He was more than out of shape, and all this physical activity was making his body ache.

CHAPTER 9

The official entrance to the Coliseum was on East Broad Street, but lately nobody ever used that one. As far as the neighborhood was concerned, the place was closed down. Major renovations had been done to ensure it was noise and light proof. No parking was allowed near the building, except for Pestilence and her Interns. Unless you knew the place was open, nobody ever went that way. Eugene gave Bob directions to park around the building in the only parking space that was marked.

Back before Texarkana expanded toward the highway, the Coliseum used to be an old department store. Eugene wasn't sure if it had been the original Sears in town, or maybe it had been JC Penney. Texarkana's original downtown, like many small town's original market areas, lost its momentum. Fortunately for the area, the locals were trying to bring it back to its old glory. Eugene was afraid they would start a boycott if they knew about their underground club.

"You guys bought this place?" Bob asked Eugene as they made their way to the backdoor.

"It was the obvious choice. After two failed attempts to turn it into a club, we figured third time was the charm," Eugene told Bob as he fixed his collar, extremely proud of himself. "The place is packed every night."

"It probably helps that you are providing your clientele with tons of illegal drugs," Bob told Eugene in a very neutral tone. Eugene couldn't believe it. Bob wasn't judging him, just pointing out the obvious.

"We figured Famine shouldn't be the only one making a profit out of his gifts," Eugene told Bob as he approached a steel door. He knocked three times in a very specific pattern.

"You don't have a key?" Bob asked, concern etched across his forehead.

"Of course I do, but club hours have started," Eugene told Bob. When he realized Bob wasn't following him, he continued. "We have massive security in place, so if I tried to open the door, I would get shot," Eugene finished.

"Isn't that a little drastic?" Bob's wide eyes darted every way they could. "Are we going to be searched?"

"We are not, but anybody else that comes here would. We allow anyone in, but we also take a lot of precautions," Eugene explained. He didn't mention that the security was also there to make sure the cops didn't bust in on them.

After a few minutes, the doors cracked opened.

"Boss, it took you long enough to get here," a short man with a shot gun told Eugene.

"Sorry, Roy. We were all the way at A&M," Eugene said. "Roy, meet Big Bob. Big Bob, meet Roy." Eugene decided to use Bob's street name for the introductions because he knew Roy had connections everywhere and probably had heard of Big Bob.

"Big Bob? *The* Big Bob that used to hang around Abuelitas?" Eugene was pleased when Roy didn't disappoint.

"I have never been referred to as 'The Big Bob' before, but yes, it's me," Bob told Roy as they shook hands with each other. "You can just call me Bob if you like."

"No way, Big Bob," Roy told him. "You are a legend around these parts. I want people to know that I know the real Big Bob. But come in, hurry." Roy stepped aside and ushered them inside the building.

"Glad you're a fan, but we need to get back to business," Eugene told Roy, bringing him back to reality. "What is going on?" He moved down one of the side corridors to look inside the club.

"Where do your customers come in?" Bob asked, his gaze taking in the empty hall.

"The crowds get bigger and bigger each night. We have two underground entrances on opposite sides of the building. You actually go through a tunnel to get here. It adds to the mystique and the kids go crazy over it," Roy answered, beaming with pride.

Eugene appreciated his private entrance. He was not that excited to walk through another underground tunnel to get here. He wanted to take full advantage of the outside world whenever he was away from the lab.

"That's creative," Bob told Roy. "Where are they?" Bob peered out a glass window Roy had taken them to. "Should I even ask if this is a one-way mirror?" Bob pointed at the glass window in front of him.

"Of course, my man." Roy smiled brightly. "It's a mirror on the other side. We have a few across the place to monitor the crowd. You would be surprise what people do in front of a mirror in a club," Roy finished, giving the mirror a mischievous look.

"I probably don't want to know," Bob told him.

"No, you really don't," Eugene confirmed.

"Over there, back of the club, two o'clock." Both Bob and Eugene looked in the direction Roy had given them.

The table Roy had pointed at had four people. From his location, he couldn't see their facial features. They were next to each other, but not talking or looking at each other. Eugene wasn't even sure they were together.

"Are you sure they are together?" Eugene asked Roy for confirmation.

"I'll put money on it. I never met four strangers that have the same dumbass tattoo on their necks," Roy told them.

"What kind of tattoo?" Eugene hadn't seen any special markings on them.

"You won't believe it, but they have paw prints. Who gets a tattoo like that?" Roy asked him. "I have to admit they are fairly concealed, and unless you were taking full inventory of them, you probably wouldn't notice. We almost missed them," he explained.

Eugene had hired Roy and his team for their top skills. They were responsible for tracking all movements in the club and watching for anything suspicious. That included any gang associations that decided to visit. Eugene appreciated their skills and their ability to keep up with everyone.

"Boss, how would you like to handle this?" Roy asked Eugene.

"Unfortunately, I need to ask our friends some questions. They have something of mine that I want back," Eugene said, and he left it at that. He wasn't going to confess to anyone else that they were missing Fourth. "We might as well get it over with." He sighed. The last thing he wanted to do was go over there, but he would do anything for Fourth.

Eugene made his way around the security door to the club. He waved at the team on duty and walked slowly toward the werewolves. Bob and Roy flanked him on both sides without seeming too menacing. The music was bumping and Eugene had the desire to start dancing. Although he had a feeling it wouldn't have the same effect as it did in the Cave.

He made it to the table after avoiding tons of drunk kids. "Good evening," Eugene said to the group.

"You!" yelled the female—the same female from the club.

Eugene didn't have time to add anything else to his statement. The female started shifting to wolf form and Eugene screamed. Before he could run away, she punched him in the face. Eugene went flying at least five feet in the air and landed on top of another group.

"Fight," somebody screamed, and with those words, the club exploded into violence.

Eugene looked around the riotous club. He had no idea where to go or what to do, but if he didn't do something, the rioting crowd would trample him to death. Except he was finding it quite difficult to breathe. In fact, he thought he might pass out at any minute, at least until he was dragged to his feet.

"Bad place to take a nap, Eugene. Let's get you out of here," Bob tugged Eugene back to the safety of the security office.

Bob was a trained soldier, which made it easy for him to clear a way through any crowd. When Bob let Eugene go, he followed behind him, keeping his head down. His face was already throbbing, and he was afraid his right eye had started to swell shut. Eugene couldn't quite see how Bob had done it, but he wondered if people were being tossed out of their way.

It didn't take them longer than five minutes to get behind the safety of the glass, and once there, Eugene leaned against the wall and held his face. Bob didn't say anything for a while. Instead, he watched as security resolved the fight.

After a few minutes, Bob said, "Eugene, those guys are good." Admiration shone from his eyes.

"They better be for the amount of money we paid them," Eugene said softly.

"Ouch." Bob sucked in a breath as he saw Eugene's face. "That's going to leave a mark tomorrow." He came closer, grabbing Eugene's chin and moving his face around.

"What are you looking for?" Eugene asked as Bob continued turning his face.

"You got punched by a werewolf. I need to make sure you didn't get scratched or anything," Bob said.

"Oh relax. It wouldn't make a difference if I was," Eugene told him. "I'm immune. Remember."

"I keep forgetting. That is one great gift to have," Bob told Eugene. "You are still going to have a black eye. I'll get you one of Eric's shakes to help with the swelling."

Eugene must look really bad for Bob to be offering him a snake.

"Tell me, how does Isis handle all this?" Eugene asked. Isis dealt with this kind of stuff on a daily basis, and it amazed him that she could still move the next day. He was already sore.

"Training. Lots and lots of training. You should join us for practice," Bob told Eugene. "You have to remember, Isis's first couple of months were brutal. She got beat up at lot, and that kept happening until she got better. We can get you there." Excitement gleamed from Bob's eyes. He was way too enthusiastic about the idea of training Eugene.

"I'll think about it," Eugene replied.

Bob opened his mouth to say something, but Roy walked into the room and saved Eugene from further discussion on the subject.

"Damn, Boss," Roy said as his gaze fell on Eugene. "It's like Mike Tyson said once, 'everyone has a plan until you get punched in the face.'"

"Information that would have been useful *before* I went out there," Eugene replied.

"How is the situation out there?" Bob asked, cutting off Eugene's complaints.

"Everything is under control, but the punks got away," Roy told Bob, looking out the glass with him.

"Boss, are you there?" a male voice came from a walkie-talkie.

"What's going on, G?" Roy replied to the speaker.

"You better get over here. I got a kid overdosing, and it's bad," G told his boss.

"Oh no. Not again," Bob said. "Eugene, stay here. I got this." Bob ran out the door with Roy leading the way.

Eugene dropped to the floor and held his face. He had no idea how fighters could handle it because his whole face hurt. He was pretty sure even his hair was aching, and the pain made it impossible to think straight. He wanted to feel bad for not helping Bob, but he was too tired to care. Eugene leaned his head back and just like that, he passed out.

CHAPTER 10

Eugene woke up with a pounding headache and a stiff neck. To make things worse, his eye was swollen shut. As he tried to sit up, a case of vertigo hit him, and Roy and Bob had to carry him to the truck. He was grateful that they at least let him get in by himself.

It was past two in the morning by the time Bob pulled into Reapers. Eugene tried to climb the stairs, but he stumbled more than anything else, so Bob helped him make his way to the top.

Being up this late made Eugene feel disgusting. He couldn't remember a time he had felt so tired, and the only time he ever stayed up this late was on the weekends when he visited Reapers. During a regular work week at the lab, the Interns had a curfew, and Eugene was normally in bed by nine. Days like today, he really missed his boring schedule. At the lab, nobody ever punched him in the face and he definitely never spent his time chasing crazy werewolves.

They entered the loft to find both Constantine and Bartholomew still up. Isis had told him that everyone at Reapers was a night owl besides her, which was crazy to Eugene.

"Holy cow, what happened?" Bartholomew shouted as soon as he saw Eugene. He ran across the room and helped Bob place Eugene gently in one of the dining chairs.

"I'm fine. It probably looks worse than it is," Eugene told Bartholomew. Hopefully they believed him, but he doubted they would.

"It looks like somebody beat the hell out of you," Constantine told him as he jumped on the kitchen table to get a better look.

"In that case, it looks exactly how I feel," Eugene admitted, ready to accept the humiliation.

"You and Isis are officially magnets for people beating you up,"

Constantine told Eugene, moving closer to his face.

"Hey now. What happened to personal space?" Eugene asked as Constantine inched even closer.

"You are an Intern. There's no such thing as personal space," Constantine told him. "Bartholomew, get the ointment from my bedroom. Bob, hand Eugene a shake and a cold patch. We will get this bruise gone in no time," he said, putting a paw on Eugene's cheek.

"Ouch," Eugene whined.

"Stop whining, Eugene. We need to get this fixed before you get permanent scars," Constantine told him.

Even with how tender his face felt, Constantine's paws were soft against it. Not that Eugene would tell him that. If he did, Constantine would probably hit him in the same spot he'd already been hit, and he really didn't need that.

"Here you go, Constantine." Bartholomew opened the ointment and slid it on the table.

"Bob, please hold Eugene down," Constantine said.

"Hold me down? What are you going to do to me?" Eugene shouted.

"Dude, you look like you got in the ring with Rocky and he destroyed you," Bartholomew told him.

"What did they hit you with, a two by four?" Constantine asked Eugene.

"It was only one punch," Eugene whined.

"One punch by a werewolf that threw him at least four feet in the air," Bob said, adding the details Eugene had purposefully left out.

"Those punks are acting like animals," Constantine told him. "You were better off getting hit by a two by four. Your entire face is swollen, which means I need to release some of the fluids building up in there." He leaned closer again.

"Oh no," Eugene said, trying to stand, but Bob held him down.

"Here." Bartholomew handed Eugene a rubber spatula.

"What's this for?" Eugene asked, not sure if he wanted to take the spatula or not.

"Put it in your mouth and bite down. It always helps Isis," Bartholomew explained.

Panic settled in Eugene's chest, but he followed the instructions Bartholomew gave him.

"Okay, take a deep breath and close your eyes," Constantine told

Eugene. "This will only take a second."

Eugene wasn't sure what to do, but as soon as he saw Constantine extending his claws, he shut his eyes.

Constantine had been right. The whole process took less than three minutes. Unfortunately for Eugene, those were the longest three minutes of his life. Bob held him down on the chair and Bartholomew squeezed his hand for moral support, but nothing helped. As soon as Constantine cut his cheek open, Eugene bit down on the spatula, but his screams still came through loud and clear. When it was over, he was still shaking.

"Eugene, you can open your eyes now," Constantine said. It took Eugene a minute to realize he wasn't being held down anymore.

"Oh wow, I can see," Eugene exclaimed as he slowly touched his face. "Wait. My head doesn't feel like it's going to explode. Constantine, you are a miracle man. I mean cat. Definitely miracle cat." Rambling was what Eugene did best, especially when he was happy. Which he was. Being pain free felt amazing.

"Breathe Eugene. We don't need you passing out with excitement," Constantine told him. "Drink your shake and keep the cold patch on for at least fifteen minutes. The rest of the swelling will go down." Constantine pointed to the two items on the table in front of Eugene.

"You are looking much better already," Bartholomew told Eugene with a smile.

"Do I want to know what's in the ointment?" Eugene asked, looking at the strange container next to Constantine. Inside was a glowing, greenish cream.

"Not at all. Even a scientist would freak out if they knew my secrets," Constantine told him with a smirk. "Let's just say this one is imported from Guatemala, and an old medicine woman makes it for me."

Eugene really wanted to meet this woman. She was good.

"Eugene, drink your shake," Bob reminded Eugene.

Eugene scrunched up his face as he glanced at the shake. It had a strange, brown hue, and even though he knew every shake was made by Eric and Isis drank one every time she got beat up, it looked more than disgusting. Of course, so did the glowing cream, but that had healed his face.

He shrugged. What did he have to lose? Holding his breath, he took one long gulp. It tasted way better than he had expected, like peanut butter and bananas.

"This isn't bad," Eugene announced with joy.

"Eric is getting more creative with his flavors after Isis complained about one of his creations," Constantine told him, rolling his eyes. "Those things cure almost everything and she still had the nerve to complain." Eugene could tell Constantine was offended, but he didn't blame Isis. Nobody wanted to drink something that looked like water pulled up from a sewer drain.

"Well, this one is good. Thank you," Eugene told Constantine as he placed the cold patch on his face. His muscles immediately relaxed and his breathing normalized.

"Besides Eugene being used as a piñata, did you guys find out anything?" Constantine narrowed his gaze on Bob.

"They are organized, and they know what they are doing." Bob's hesitant tone made sense. Nobody wanted to give werewolves that kind of credit.

"Tell me about it," Bartholomew told him. "They executed synchronized deliveries in over ten locations. I have no idea how many people are in this gang, but they are all over the town." Bartholomew shook his head.

"That's the odd part," Constantine jumped in. "Traditionally in a pack, you don't have more than eight to ten members. Based on their patterns, they have at least thirty people working together." He scratched his face.

"What's the big deal about that?" Eugene asked as he switched hands to hold his cold patch.

"To organize such an attack in all those locations and with that many people, you need a really strong Alpha," Constantine told him. "We would have noticed somebody that strong."

"We would have? How?" Bartholomew asked, and everyone's eyes went to Constantine.

"Texarkana has other shifters in town," Constantine explained. "A strong alpha would try to dominate and take over a territory. We haven't even had a scrimmage. That doesn't make any sense," he concluded.

"So we have an organized gang of werewolves that is also mysterious and unconventional. What else could go wrong?" Eugene asked.

"Let's not tempt fate. We got plenty of problems already," Bob told Eugene as he started making coffee. "Have you heard from

Isis?" he asked.

"I'm telling you, she is taking a vacation at the bed and breakfast," Constantine told him.

"She called and confirmed she would be staying at least three nights over there," Bartholomew added.

"I agree with the boss. She is chilling in Jefferson," Bob said with a smile.

Constantine and Bob nodded their heads to each other.

"At least somebody is having a good time," Eugene said. "What is our next move? I'm tired of running around Texarkana stabbing people." If only they knew how much he meant those words. He had to be looking crazy doing what he'd been doing.

"I got the number for our little kidnappers from Seventh. We are going to set up a drop point for tomorrow," Constantine told him.

"Are you serious? We can't pay them. The Mistress would kill us." Eugene tried to get up from his chair and panic shoved him into motion, but he got stuck.

"Calm down, Eugene. You're going to hurt yourself again," Bob told him as he slid Constantine a mug of coffee, then handed a hot chocolate to Bartholomew.

"Can I get one?" Eugene asked Bob, staring at Bartholomew's mug and licking his lips. Bob made the best hot chocolate in the country.

"As soon as you are done with your shake," Bob replied.

"Are you done freaking out?" Constantine asked. "Of course we aren't negotiating with kidnappers. Especially those punks. But we still need to get them out in the open." He licked his face after sipping his coffee. "We have our own policies for dealing with these types of situations. Not nearly as dramatic as yours."

"What should I do?" Eugene asked as he finished his shake. Before he even set his glass down, Bob gave him a mug of hot chocolate.

"Sleep," Bob answered for Constantine. "It's way past your bedtime and you are delirious."

"No, I'm not," Eugene said, stifling a giggle that snuck right out of his throat.

Constantine angled his head towards him. "Says the man bouncing around in his chair at the sight of hot chocolate."

"But it's so good. And it's hot, and silky, and *so* good." He was delirious. More than delirious. He'd lost every marble he'd collected in his head and thrown them so far away he had no chance of collecting them.

"Got it. It's so good," Constantine told him. "Bob, please help Giggles to bed."

"With pleasure, Boss. I will be back to debrief shortly," Bob told Constantine as he tried to assist Eugene out of his chair.

"Eugene, don't listen to him. You are right. It is so good," Bartholomew told Eugene as he started to do his own happy dance by his computer station.

"Bob, we really need to talk about the ingredients you use for your hot chocolate," Constantine told Bob as he gave Eugene and Bartholomew a suspicious look.

"Of course, Boss," Bob answered, then he walked Eugene out of the loft.

"I could've handled getting to your room on my own," Eugene told Bob as they headed down the stairs.

"Probably, but you forgot your cold patch leaving the table," Bob told him as he held up the compressed patch.

"I couldn't hold the chocolate and the patch at the same time," Eugene confessed. "It's all about priorities." He took another sip from his mug and felt like everything was right in the world.

"At least you have your priorities straight," Bob told him as he inched Eugene into the room.

Eugene had a feeling he'd be out as soon as his head hit his pillow.

CHAPTER 11

ugene laid in a giant tub filled with hot chocolate, with giant marshmallows floating all around him. The tub sat between some trees in what looked like the heart of a forest. Instead of bubbles in his bath, there were layers and layers of cream. The rich aroma of chocolate wrapped around him and his mouth watered in anticipation. Just as he started sliding down to immerse himself in the goodness, the vision evaporated into dust.

It had all been a dream. A beautiful, glorious dream.

"Eugene, stop making funny faces and wake up," a familiar voice told him, and it sounded like he was far away.

Where was he? He had no idea what had happened, but he thought he was in a bed. He felt below him, still not opening his eyes all the way.

"Wake up, Eugene," Bob shouted as he shook Eugene's shoulders.

"No! My chocolate!" Eugene shouted before opening his eyes.

"Do I want to know what you were dreaming about?" Bob asked Eugene.

"Probably not, but it was delicious," Eugene answered, still smelling the hot chocolate in the air.

"Are you looking for this?" Bob asked him as he held out an even bigger mug filled to the brim with hot chocolate.

"How did you know?" Eugene asked, grabbing the cup and taking a huge gulp. He didn't care that he hadn't brushed his teeth yet. After his dream, he craved the sweet deliciousness inside the mug.

"Easy. You have the same look Constantine gets when he is smelling his favorite dish," Bob said, eyeing Eugene. "I could make a fortune just charging you and Isis for this stuff." He laughed, but he shouldn't have. He was probably right.

"And Bartholomew. You can't forget him," Eugene replied.

"Of course. We can't forget Bartholomew," Bob told him, chuckling.

"What's going on? Why am I getting breakfast in bed? This is not normal," Eugene asked Bob after his mind finally cleared.

"We need more antidote," Bob told Eugene. "After last night, everyone is out. To make things worse, we need it ASAP to head to the high school." Bob's smile morphed into a frown.

"What's going on at the high school? Aren't they on summer break?" Eugene asked. It had been a few years since he graduated from high school, but he was sure school didn't go all year long.

"Yes, the regular year is out, but they have summer classes going now," Bob clarified. "They spotted a few of the werewolves at the campus and the police locked down the school. They are afraid of another incident like A&M."

"That's a good call," Eugene told him as he forced himself out of bed. "I think we are out of supplies, though. Even EpiPens." He glanced up at the ceiling as he made a mental inventory of what they had left.

"Way ahead of you," Bob said. "We sent Shorty to your lab to get more supplies. Hurry, we need you," he added from the doorway.

Eugene moved. He jumped in the shower, waking himself up even more, and as he dressed he realized he had just as many personal things in this room as he did at the lab. Eugene wondered when Reapers had turned into his extended home, but he didn't have a lot of time to ponder that thought.

Ten minutes later, Eugene crossed the first floor of Reapers and entered his makeshift lab. Eugene was surprised to find Shorty, Constantine, and Second in the lab, especially since he'd only been expecting Bob.

"Second, what are you doing here? Am I in trouble?" Eugene's heart rate beat like the wings of a hummingbird. Did Pestilence know what happened? If she found out, he was a dead man.

"I'm here to help," Second told Eugene with a smile.

"Really?" Eugene asked, his voice high pitched with surprise.

"I know how hard it is to be the rookie in the lab, but we are family," Second told Eugene. "You don't have to do this alone." He beamed with enthusiasm.

"Not to mention, two mad scientists are faster than one," Constantine told them. "I'm all about this. Now get to work."

"You are one demanding guardian," Second told Constantine. "Are you sure you never worked for the Mistress?" Second's gaze burned into Constantine.

Constantine scoffed with disgust. "Work for that hag? I would rather die." His lip curled towards his nose

"Boss, are you okay?" Bob asked Constantine.

"Even thinking about her makes me sick," Constantine announced.

"That would be a no to your question, Second," Bob translated for Constantine.

"That's a shame. You would be awesome in the lab," Second told Constantine, his eyes looking a little sad.

"This sounds like a great family reunion, but do you all still need me?" Shorty finally asked. Left to his own devices, he'd been playing with Eugene's chemistry beakers in the back.

"Second, did you bring enough supplies to make at least five hundred pens?" Eugene asked his peer.

"We have enough for double that," Second said, and his chest puffed with pride.

"Then we are good. Thank you, my man," Eugene told Shorty, shaking his hand.

"Anytime, E," Shorty told him. "Now hurry. We need as much of that vaccine as you can make. After last night, we are all out. Big Bob, I'm out." He shot out the door.

"Keep me posted if any more cases pop up," Bob told Shorty, who turned and saluted him before he vanished. "Okay gentlemen, do you need me for anything?" Bob asked.

"I think we are good here," Eugene answered.

"Perfect. I'm going to make breakfast." Bob announced and headed out the door.

"Oh wow, I get to have the famous Bob's breakfast," Second said, almost giddy. "The guys are going to be so jealous." He looked like a kid in a candy store.

"You guys really need to get out more often," Constantine told both Interns. "You are starting to scare me." He headed out the door but stopped before walking out. "By the way, Shorty brought back several samples of the food the werewolves were using to distribute the drugs. Do you guys want it?"

"Yes," both men answered in unison.

"That is perfect. We can see if they are diluting the stuff with anything," Eugene told Constantine.

"Great. It's in the box in the corner. Now don't have too much fun in here." Constantine left both scientists to play with their toys.

"They are just going to leave us unsupervised?" Second asked Eugene.

"Pretty much," Eugene answered, realizing Death's team was a lot more trusting than Pestilence. If you were given access to Reapers, you had unlimited access. Unlike their lab, where everyone had restricted access based on their clearance level. Their worlds were very different. "Second, how did you get permission to come and help me?" Eugene knew how difficult it was to leave the lab.

"Seventh sent me," Second said, smiling wide. "He told the rest of the crew he needed me to assist you in the distribution of a new food virus to affect the city for the holidays. According to Seventh, he created it himself and wanted to see how many people could ingest it, and what the consequences would be," Second finished, then he brought the box of samples to their work station.

"That is brilliant," Eugene admitted. "Where did he get that idea from?" he asked, more than impressed with Seventh's ingenuity.

"He drilled poor Shorty on the status of the situation. Once he got all the facts, he created his own cover story." Second gave Eugene an impressive nod. "I shouldn't be surprised how creative Seventh can be. I heard stories that he was a wild one in his youth. Rumor has it, he even seduced the Mistress into giving him the job."

Eugene froze at that announcement. "Do you believe that?"

"Hell yeah," Second answered.

That caught Eugene off guard. Second had never been very forthcoming with information, so having him tell him this shocked Eugene. Maybe Reapers had an odd effect on Interns that did not work for Death.

"How can you be so sure?" Eugene asked, wanting to hear more of the lab's drama.

"Everyone knows Seventh is the favorite. He can say and do whatever he wants, even though he is not the senior one," Second told him. "According to Maria, our senior cook, who is at least ninety years old, she said Seventh was a looker when he was younger. He is still pretty smooth, like a classic Sean Connery." He smirked.

Eugene didn't know what to say, but he liked hearing all the gossip.

"I can't believe it," Eugene mumbled.

"None of those guys are perfect, they just pretend for your sake," Second confessed. "You were still young in our ways so they were trying to mold you as much as they could."

"They were? Does that mean they stopped?" Eugene worried his team had given up on him, or that they would be sending him away.

"We all realized you are not helpless or a mindless puppy that can be brainwashed." Second told Eugene. "You were the fifth rookie we recruited, and you haven't let us down." He met Eugene's eyes.

Eugene frowned. "What happened to the other four?" Eugene had no idea there were others before him.

"They were textbook brilliant, but lacked imagination," Second answered as he organized the beakers. "They brought nothing new to the team." He stopped to look at Eugene again. "You are different. Besides being curious, you have this innate ability to make friends. You also aren't scared of bending the rules for the greater good. Eugene, you have opened a bridge between Death and us that has been closed for decades. That is huge."

Eugene's jaw dropped open. He hadn't even realized Second knew his name. "I didn't think anyone noticed." His voice cracked as he leaned against the worktable for support. "I just keep making mistakes."

"Of course you are making mistakes. That just means you are working. You are experimenting and testing boundaries," Second told him in a proud voice. "We are scientists, Eugene. We suck at expressing feelings. But the lab is lonely when you are not around. Yes, everyone is excited when Sunday rolls around, and it's not because you are bringing ice cream or dessert from Reapers. It's because *you* are coming home."

Eugene swallowed hard around the lump wedged in his throat. "I thought I drove everyone nuts and you guys were happy when I wasn't there."

"We are all creatures of habit. You know that more than anyone," Second told him and Eugene nodded in agreement. "You are that rare one that turns the lab upside down. When you are around, there's music playing, food cooking, and all sorts of chaos. We haven't seen that in years. You brought life and youth back to the lab. So, no, we notice when you are gone and we are not letting you fail," he told Eugene and gave him a fist bump. "Welcome to the rebel society."

"The what?" Eugene asked.

"Oh, come on. You know we have a few brown nosers in the group," Second answered. "We are the group that keeps the balance in the force, else the Mistress would be total banshee crazy." He winked at Eugene and started organizing things again.

"What side of the force are we?" Eugene asked, loving the Star Wars reference.

"It depends on the day. Today we are the dark side," Second told Eugene. "It's time to start showing you some tricks, though. You ready to learn, Grasshopper?" he asked Eugene as he made beakers disappears. "You didn't think it was only Death that gave her Interns magic?" He waved his hands in front of his body and sparks flashed around.

"How come I didn't know this before?" Eugene asked with wide eyes.

"We needed to figure out what type of Intern you were going to be," Second told him. "Going against the rules for the greater good answered our questions. Proud of you, Rookie. Ready?" He grinned as the experiments he'd been working on levitated.

"I'm all in," Eugene answered. He loved his job, but there had been so many times he had felt like an outsider. This was the first time he finally felt like he belonged.

CHAPTER 12

Less than two hours later, Second and Eugene entered the loft. Bob was serving eggs and bacon to Bartholomew, who still looked half asleep. There was a plate of bacon in front of Constantine, and he was devouring it.

"Are you guys okay? Do we need more supplies?" Constantine asked.

"We are done," Eugene announced with a cheerful lilt.

"What? How?" Bob asked. "Last batch took you almost five hours."

"Constantine was right. Two worked better one," Eugene answered with a shrug.

"I know. I'm always right. But unless you two conjured potions out of thin air, that is a miracle," Constantine told them, giving both a suspicious look.

Maybe Constantine didn't know about their magic. But he had to, right? He was older than dirt, after all.

"You said it was an emergency, so we made it happen," Eugene told Constantine with a smile.

"I'll take the miracle because we need it," Bob told them.

"What happened?" Second asked.

"Sit down and get something to eat while I explain," Bob told him. "This is going to be a long, busy day, so you better get as much food as you can while you have the chance."

Eugene licked his lips and Second rubbed his hands together as Bob brought out a quiche from the oven, as well as bacon, toast, and fresh juice.

"When did you have time to make all this?" Second asked Bob.

"You are not the only one with magic tricks, child," Constantine told Eugene, and after a quick glance at Second, both of them gave the cat a wide-eyed stare. "Bob has skills we don't even know about," he finished between mouthfuls.

So, he did know.

"You should try these eggs. They are seriously amazing," Bartholomew told the men. "Last week he made eggs-in-a-hole with gluten free bread." His eyes shone as he ate his breakfast.

"What are eggs-in-a-hole?" Second asked, looking between Bartholomew and Bob.

"It's an egg that gets fried in the middle of a slide of bread," Bob answered while he cut his quiche. "I was afraid the quiche would be cold by the time you two were done, but nice timing," he told them, giving each a huge slice.

Second didn't wait a second before grabbing his fork and diving in. After he chewed it up and swallowed, he said, "This is divine. Mr. Bob, you just made my month. I'm in heaven." The words came out of him as if he were singing them with joy.

"You should skip the bacon then, or you might die of happiness. Let me help you out," Constantine joked as he reached for Second's plate. Second stuffed two slides in his mouth, which made his cheeks bulge out like a chipmunk storing nuts. Constantine laughed and shook his head.

"Thank you, Bob. This is amazing," Eugene said as he let the flavors float in his mouth before he swallowed them down.

"I'm glad, but hurry and eat. We need to get going," Bob told them.

"What is going on?" Second asked.

"We intercepted a police report. One of the students at the high school just went postal," Bartholomew told them.

"What do you mean by postal?" Second asked.

"He is holding the rest of the students hostage," Bartholomew continued. "According to the officer, the kid was mumbling about seeing ghosts and demons everywhere."

"Would it be possible for your drugs to force a person's third eye to open?" Constantine asked.

"We have never seen that happen, but it doesn't mean it isn't possible," Second answered. "Of course, he could just be hallucinating. It depends how strong the dose was."

"It was probably a really high dose," Eugene jumped in. "The ones we found in the other carriers all varied in strength. It's like they are experimenting with different amounts and mixtures." Eugene stabbed at his quiche. He couldn't be more annoyed that the werewolves were doing this.

"Any ideas how we are going to get passed a police blockade?" Bob asked the dynamic duo.

"I brought our IDs with me," Second said with a huge grin.

"What ID are you carrying that has you smiling like a diabolical dog?" Constantine asked Second.

"The most important one. The get out of jail free card," Second replied.

Constantine pressed his lips together and nodded. "You have IRS badges with you? I'm impressed."

Second frowned. "Not nearly as good as that." He turned to Eugene. "We really need to get a couple of those."

"I'll take second best. What do you have?" Bob asked Second.

"CDC ID cards. What every scientist needs to get anywhere," Second announced.

"Those worked great last time," Bartholomew said. "Are you hitting the city quarantine again?" Excitement came from him in waves.

"Not this time. They should get us inside the school without a problem, though," Second told them. "Do you still have your knock out serum here?" he asked Eugene.

"We have it by the pounds," Eugene told him.

"Good, we will probably need some," Second told them, then continued explaining. "If the students are turning hostile instead of overdosing, that means they changed something in the formula. We will need to knock them out before administering the antidote or they will be too dangerous to control." His eyes landed on Bob as he finished.

"That sounds like a great plan," Bob told them. "I'm all about them being asleep before trying to stab them. I'll get the paint guns ready. Meet you both at the truck." He turned and headed out the door.

"Too bad we couldn't enjoy our breakfast longer," Second told the group, putting his fork down.

"Take it with you," Bartholomew told him. "That's what we do with Isis or else she would never eat. Grab a to-go container and a drink." He pointed at the cabinets for Second.

Second was bouncing for joy as he ran towards the cabinet. He grabbed a container with a lid and shoveled his breakfast inside.

"At least you have great taste in food." Constantine grinned at

Second.

After getting their meals ready, both men ran out the door to meet Bob. The last thing Eugene wanted to do was keep Bob waiting.

In less than fifteen minutes, the team arrived at Texas High School on Summerhill Road. The police had the grounds surrounded. Eugene had no idea how they were going to get near the school.

After Bob parked across the street, the three of them jogged back.

"I really hope you have a plan," Bob told Eugene and Second.

"We have something," Second confessed. "I'm just not sure it constitutes as a plan."

The men made their way towards the police line. Three officers stopped them from progressing. Bob's eyes shifted to the right, and Eugene followed him to find Eric. It looked like he was about to head towards the group, but Bob jerked his head in silent negation, which made Eric turn around and ignore them.

"Gentlemen, this area is restricted. You need to clear out now," one of the officers told them. He looked older than the rest and had an air of authority about him. Eugene had no idea what any of their ranks were, but he had a feeling this guy was high on the list.

"Good morning, Sir. Glad to finally find you," Second told the men in a brisk, nasally voice. "We have a situation here," he said in a serious tone.

Eugene scrunched his eyebrows. How had he changed his voice like that so quickly?

"Yes, thank you. We figured that out all of our own," the officer replied, sarcasm dripping from his words.

"You don't understand, Sir. We are from the CDC and this town has been under observation since last May," Second told the officer, taking a deliberate pause to let the facts sink in.

"This is not another zombie attack, right?" He shot Second a worried look.

"That's what we are here to figure out," Second replied. "We are highly trained for this type of situation. We need to get in."

Eugene stood there in amazement. The poor officer was terrified, which meant Second had done his job and he'd done it well.

"Sure thing." The officer's voice shivered. "We will clear a path for you."

"No need, young man. Just let us know where the students are located," Second told the officer.

Eugene raised his chin, trying to look as focused and professional as possible. When he glanced at Bob, he was doing the same.

"They are in the library." The officer pointed to a building to the left of the main entrance. "You can enter through the building. The outside doors are locked from the inside," he added, shaking his head.

"Thank you, good man. We will take the outside door," Second informed them as he led the team towards the library.

"I hope you have a plan for breaking in," Bob told Second.

"That part is easy. Getting close to the library without him seeing us might be a little trickier," Second told them as he stopped and analyzed the building.

"I can help with that part," Eugene told Bob and Second. "Bob, you still have your grenade launcher?" Eugene asked Bob.

"I never leave home without it," Bob told Eugene as he pulled off his backpack. He lifted a retractable grenade launcher from inside and handed Eugene the weird device.

"Thank you," Eugene told Bob as he took out the grenade-sized balls from his own backpack.

"What are you carrying with you?" Second asked, examining the odd-looking bubbles.

"I have been wanting to paint my room, but I'm too lazy to do it by hand," Eugene explained. "I created giant paint balls that automatically spread out when shot on a wall."

"Rookie, that is brilliant. Why are you not using them?" Second looked at Eugene expectantly.

"I have never tested them," Eugene admitted.

"Sounds like today is a great time to do so," Bob told Eugene, taking the launcher and the experiment. Before Eugene could protest, Bob fired on the building.

The result was not what Eugene expected. Bob had excellent aim and hit the blasts right in the middle. Within seconds, the formula spread all over the wall and glass.

"I'm pretty sure they won't be able to see us," Bob told the scientist.

"Let's hope the school doesn't sue us. I have no clue how to get that stuff off," Eugene admitted, not meeting anyone's eyes.

"Let's worry about that later. One problem at a time," Bob answered and pulled out his paint gun.

All three men ran across the grass area doing military maneuvers. Eugene was grateful for Bob's dedication. He did not want to get killed by a kid today. When they made it to the door, Bob covered them. Second took a small syringe from his lab pocket.

"What is that?" Eugene asked.

"Acid," Second replied.

"Do you normally carry acid in your pockets?" Eugene asked Second, taking a few steps back.

"As you get older, you will be surprised how handy this stuff can be," Second told Eugene.

Second sprayed the lock's core, as well as the door handle. Within seconds, the metal in both areas disintegrated. Eugene was impressed, and Bob nodded in agreement. Before either scientist could move, Bob wrenched the door open and rushed in. Eugene and Second followed close behind.

Eugene paused, taking in the sight before him. A group of students were huddle in a corner crying. One tall student stood over the group, holding a bat above their heads.

"Get out, warrior," the student screamed right before he charged at Bob.

Bob didn't hesitate. He shot the student in the chest. In a way, Eugene felt bad for the kid because he hadn't stood a chance. Bob was an accurate shooting machine who did not miss, and within three minutes, all hostiles were contained.

"Damn, you are good," Second told Bob.

"Plenty of practice," he said plainly. He wasn't bragging, just stating a fact. "Now what?"

"We administer the antidote and check the rest of the students," Second told him. "If they are showing signs, they get the antidote. We have to make sure nobody is infected." Second glanced around the library as he spoke.

"Sounds like a plan. I'll go get the cops while you guys to that." Bob ran out of the library before either man could answer.

"Is he always that intense?" Second asked Eugene.

"Nope, normally that's Isis's job," Eugene told him. "You take the left side; I'll take the right." He pointed towards his side.

"Let's fix this now," Second said, and they moved, checking each student and giving them the antidote.

The police had the campus cleared within thirty minutes. All the students were brought to the library for a healthy inspection. Bob had volunteered to help the police while Eugene and Second ran their tests. Fortunately, only ten out of one hundred students had been infected. Eugene was grateful for that little miracle.

"Boys, we got to go," Bob told Second and Eugene.

"What now?" Eugene asked, hearing the urgency in Bob's tone.

"Shorty called. There's another situation at the water park," Bob told them.

"Oh no, that sounds awful," Second said.

Eugene and Bob picked up most of their tools and headed towards the library door. Second followed closely behind.

"We are all set. The officer will call me if anything else happens," Second told Bob and Eugene as they rushed to the truck.

CHAPTER 13

It didn't take the team anytime to reach the water park behind the convention center on the Arkansas side. Eugene was always confused why both the Texas and Arkansas sides decided they both needed their own convention center. Instead of making two medium size centers, they could have made a large one that would've fit thousands of people. The Reaper team all pretty much felt the same. Especially Bartholomew, but it was a sour topic for him because he'd been hoping for an arena-sized center so concerts could take place there.

Bob drove around the center and pulled right in front of the water park. People were running all over the place, screaming, and bumping into each other. The gate to the park was hanging open and there were kids everywhere. This place used to be the happening summer spot, at least until the werewolves attacked it.

"Do we really need to go out there?" Second asked from the back seat. Eugene turned around to face him and realized Second looked a little pale.

"We got this," Eugene told him, pumping a fist in the air.

"I don't know. These are little kids, Rookie," Second told him. "Kids scare me." It might have just been Eugene, but he could've sworn Second's face was a little green around the edges.

"Yes, and they will be dead kids if we don't help," Bob told both Interns. "If we don't do something now, Death will be here in no time," he reminded them as he jumped off the truck.

"Are you going to be okay?" Eugene asked Second.

"No, but I will have to be," Second replied honestly. "Bob is right. We don't have time." With a shrug, he followed Bob outside.

As they got near the park, a horrible thought struck Eugen, making him take a step back and analyze things in a different light. He understood his job at the lab, but for the first time, he felt conflicted. He'd never really thought about kids being affected by his experiments, but he couldn't ignore the fact any longer. They were targets, and they didn't deserve to be. Instead, they deserved a chance at living before judgment day.

Eugene followed Second, carrying a full bag of antidote. The situation was bad, and there was no way to sugarcoat it. Inside the park was the worst, and as he ran in, he found Bob already working on a young girl. Her pale skin told Eugene all he needed to know and thank goodness Bob was with her. He administered the antidote, then bent his ear to her mouth to make sure she was breathing.

"Big Bob, over here," Shorty yelled over the crowd.

Bob secured the young girl and took off at full speed. He leaped over lounge chairs like a professional sprinter. Eugene was amazed. Bob was in better shape than most eighteen year olds.

Eugene followed Bob at a much slower pace. Shorty was between two maniac teens. They were attacking everyone and throwing things at people, including chairs.

"Shorty, duck," Bob yelled as he pulled his paint gun from his pocket and fired while he was still running. Eugene couldn't believe it, Bob actually hit both teenagers.

Eugene made a mental note to himself: next laser tag game they played, Bob was on his team. Isis was a great marksman, but Bob had style. If he was going to be hanging out at Reapers, he needed to start taking lessons. This group was lethal.

"Shorty, hurry. Hit them," Bob shouted at Shorty.

Shorty turned around and kicked the closest kid with his boot.

"What was that for?" Bob asked him as he came to a stop next to Shorty.

"You said to hit him," Shorty explained, pointing at the kid.

"With the antidote, Shorty," Bob clarified, rubbing his temples.

"In Shorty's defense, you didn't say that," Eugene jumped in.

"Good looking out, E," Shorty told Eugene and they gave each other a fist bump.

"Fine, next time I'll be more specific. Don't kick the casualties," Bob told both Eugene and Shorty in a stern voice.

"Got it," Shorty replied with a salute.

Eugene shot both kids with the antidote. "How many kids have been trying to fight today?" he asked, trying to see if there was any kind of pattern.

"These two are the first ones," Shorty told him. "What is the plan in this situation?"

"From now on, if you find any crazy ones like these, knock them out first and then tag them," Bob told Shorty.

"Ideally, if we can reduce their chances of hurting themselves, it would be great. It would be even better if we could stop them from hurting anyone else," Eugene answered.

"Make that four people fighting," Shorty told Eugene as he pointed to another pair of kids on the far side of a pool. "Let's go, Big Bob." Both men took off running towards the pair.

Eugene had just finished checking vital signs when he heard a loud splash behind him. He turned around to find a comatose child, maybe four, in the pool, and they were sinking fast. Without thinking, Eugene jumped in the pool to get the child. It was harder than he thought. The kid was maybe forty pounds, but it was dead weight. He barely managed to get the kid to the edge in time for Second to help pull the kid out.

"There has to be an easier way of doing this," Second told him as he dragged the child to dry ground.

"If you find one, please share it with me," Eugene told Second, then he climbed out of the pool. Water avalanched off him, pouring from his soaked clothes.

"He isn't breathing," Second told him.

"Hurry, give him CPR," Eugene told Second as he made his way toward the kid.

"Rookie, I don't know how," Second told him, the words rushing out in his panic.

"Don't worry, I got him," Eugene told him. "Just give me some space." He kneeled next to the unconscious child, then tilted the child's head back and opened his mouth to clear his airways. That was when he found the piece of caramel lodged in his throat.

"Second, hurry. Administer the antidote while I start CPR." Eugene proceeded to give him mouth to mouth respirations and started chest compressions. When he was in college, taking CPR had been a joke—an easy elective. Now he was grateful for the training.

"Done," Second shouted, and right on cue, the small child started coughing. Eugene fell back, landing on his butt, but he didn't care. He was too relieved to care.

"I don't think we have time for a break," Second told Eugene.

Everywhere Eugene looked, there seemed to be another teenager having a seizure. There were so many of them, but not nearly enough of him. He didn't want to leave the little boy alone, either.

"Help, over here," Second cried.

"What are you doing?" Eugene asked.

"We need more able bodies," Second told him. "We got a crowd of people just staring at us over there. Let's put them to work." Eugene couldn't see where Second was pointing, but he heard people running towards them.

Over twenty people rushed in their direction. It was the staff from the hotel—everyone from the maintenance crew to the cleaning staff. Eugene couldn't believe it. In most cities, people would go out of their way to avoid helping each other. But in this small town, they were coming in waves to assist.

"What can we do?" a young lady in her mid-twenties asked.

"Can you get us more people?" Second asked.

Another lady nodded. "I know the staff from the other hotels. I'll go get them." She ran off.

"Great. The rest of you, we need to secure these kids and administer the antidote. Go in pairs and get them ready," Second ordered the crowd and they all dispersed.

In less than twenty minutes, with their new team of assistants, they had contained the situation. Children and teenagers alike were scattered all over the park. Each were being watched over by one of the caring souls who had volunteered. They made sure none of their patients puked on themselves or stopped breathing.

Eugene sighed. He didn't know what to do. The situation was spinning out of control and they weren't getting any closer to finding the werewolves.

He slowly walked towards the truck, hoping to dry himself with the sun. Out of the corner of his eye, Eugene saw movement. He turned around to find the female werewolf from the club—the same one who'd hit him. Without thinking, he rushed at her. The girl was leaning against a car with a grin on her face, as if she was enjoying the drama she'd created. Then she turned to face Eugene.

"Really, little boy? You don't learn, do you," she said, still smirking.

"What is wrong with you?" Eugene shouted at her, his hands clenched and shaking at his sides.

"Nothing. I just don't like humans. Not my fault your drugs are so good," she told him with a laugh.

Eugene couldn't stop himself. He threw a punch, and he almost fell over as he did. But he missed by a mile.

"You need practice," the girl told him, laughing. "I'm glad your face recovered so quickly. It would be a shame to permanently damage such a beautiful specimen."

The girl gave Eugene a kick to the chest and he went flying backwards, landing flat on his back on the ground. He tried to get up, but she'd knocked the air right out of him. He hunched over, trying to catch his breath.

"Bye, handsome," The girl waved, then hopped in her car.

Eugene rolled over with both his chest and pride injured.

"Eugene, are you okay?" Bob shouted as he came running with Shorty and Second in tow.

"E, what were you thinking taking on that chick all by yourself?" Shorty asked him while Bob and he helped Eugene to his feet. "I saw that girl take on five guys at one time and she destroyed them."

Eugene gave Shorty a wide-eyed glance. "Now you tell me."

"How was I supposed to know you were going to go all *Mortal Combat* on her ass?" Shorty asked him. "You are the sensible one in the group. That's the kind of stuff Isis would do," he said, inspecting him for injuries.

"Nice job, Rookie. I was impressed," Second told him.

They climbed in the truck and headed towards Reapers. This day was not going as well as Eugene had hoped.

"By the way, nice throw," Bob told Eugene. "If she was human, you would have taken her out. We need to work on your speed and dodging, then you will be in top fighting shape," Bob told Eugene.

"Thanks," Eugene replied. He liked the idea of being able to hold his own. "I will take you up on that offer and start training with you guys." Might as well. Bob and Isis had offered to train him on multiple occasions. At the time, he had never seen the need, although part of his hesitancy was from embarrassment. Isis was so much better than him, so he didn't want her to laugh when he sucked. After this week, he didn't care. Eugene was ready to take care of himself and his friends.

"I think we can take off now," Bob told the group. "We need to stop by Reapers and get Eugene dry clothes and regroup. Shorty, keep patrolling and report if you find anything," Bob told Shorty.

"Will do Big Bob," Shorty replied and took off for his truck.

"Aren't you glad you had a big breakfast?" Bob told both Interns as they headed towards the truck.

"At this rate, I'm sure I have burned all the calories I ate," Eugene told Bob, who only smiled in response.

CHAPTER 14

The boys were quiet all the way back to Reapers. Everyone was lost in their own thoughts. It had been a long day already and it wasn't even noon yet. Eugene was staring at his hands, afraid to look out the window. He was sure if he did, he would only see overdosed kids.

He was grateful when they made it back to Reapers, although he wasn't ready to face Constantine and tell him he failed again.

After clearing all the securities, Bob parked Storm in its assigned space. Second jumped out of the truck, full of energy. Eugene, on the other hand, dragged himself out.

"Oh wow," Second said in a high-pitched tone. "That was insane. I have not seen that kind of action in decades. What am I saying? I have never seen that much action. Not ever. We need to get ready. I'm going to make more antidote." He took off running for the lab without waiting for an answer.

"Is he always that excited?" Bob asked Eugene.

"Never," Eugene replied. "Then again, I'm finding out that I really don't know my peers as well as I'd thought. So this could be his normal self and I didn't know it," he told Bob as he stared in the direction of the lab.

"Eugene, what's the matter?" Bob asked him, concern etched into his words.

"She got away again," Eugene whispered, looking at the floor. "Things like that wouldn't happen to Isis." It was time for a pity party, and he needed to cut it out.

"Are we talking about the same Isis?" Bob asked Eugene.

"Of course. How many people named Isis do you know?" Eugene met Bob's eyes.

"The Isis I know is a work in progress, and although we love her, she is nowhere near perfect," Bob told Eugene. "For the first six months on the job, she got beat up left and right." Eugene gave Bob an incredulous look. "Isis is a musician, a fact you already know, but it took her a while to get used to her new role. She never gave up, though, regardless of how much she hated it. Every situation is not going to go perfect; the catch is to learn from them and get better." His features softened.

"I guess I never thought about it that way," Eugene answered.

"Take a shower and get some clean clothes. You will feel much better," Bob told Eugene. "I'll go brief the boss." Eugene nodded at Bob and watched him head towards the loft. Bob and Isis were both prior military, so they hadn't lost their soldier tendencies. Reporting back with an update was one of them.

Eugene headed inside Bob's apartment with his shoulders slumped. He stepped inside the apartment and flicked the light switch on.

"Hi Eugene," Death said.

Eugene screamed like a little girl who just had her favorite doll stolen.

"I'm so sorry that I startled you," Death told Eugene, trying to hide a smile.

"Are you trying to take me to my final home?" Eugene asked Death with his hand over his heart. "I think I had a heart attack. Maybe not, but I might've peed my pants," he confessed.

"Those are your only options?" Death asked.

"Oh, I'm sure I have more, but they aren't polite enough to say out loud," Eugene told Death, finally making eye contact.

Death always scared the hell out of Eugene. He saw Death as a tall man, with dark hair and dark eyes that resembled a strict school principal or angry librarian. Eugene had no idea why, since Isis explained that for her Death was a beautiful woman. Eugene wondered why he couldn't get the beautiful woman instead of the angry man.

"Are you breathing again?" Death asked Eugene, rising from the couch and fixing his suit. Death always had incredible tailored suits. That's one thing his version and Isis's had in common: the clothes were exquisite.

"I think so but I'm not sure for how much longer," Eugene confessed. He had never had a private visit from Death before.

"I'm not here to collect you," Death told him.

"I'm confused then," Eugene said.

"Why did you save that child?" Death asked Eugene.

Eugene wasn't sure how to reply. He took a deep breath before trying. "He was an innocent little boy. He didn't deserve to suffer like that," he told Death.

"But you are okay with adults dying?" Death asked Eugene, making him uncomfortable.

Eugene shrugged. "I guess." He had never thought about it. "I don't really want people to die." And as soon as the words left his mouth, he realized he actually meant them.

"Why do you work for Pestilence then?" Death asked, and that was the question he'd been avoiding asking himself.

"I don't know," Eugene blurted.

"You do know. Why Eugene?" Death pressed him.

"I like doing experiments. I just never thought about the consequences of those experiments." The truth made him feel selfish, and that upset him more than anything else.

"Eugene, we all have a purpose and path in this existence," Death told Eugene. "You are a gifted scientist, hence the reason Pestilence recruited you. You can work for her and still have your boundaries," he explained.

"How?" Eugene asked, raising his eyebrows.

"Same way you target what groups you pick. Avoid groups with children," Death answered.

"Wouldn't the Mistress get mad?" Eugene asked, sure if he did that he'd get fired.

"Pestilence can be difficult and demanding, but she also understands humanity," Death told him. "Talk to your peers. You will discover that each of them have a soft spot for something. That's how she balances the lab."

Eugene really needed to pay more attention to his people.

"Is that why you are here? To give me a pep talk," Eugene asked.

"Sometimes Interns need confirmation that they are on the right path," Death told him.

"Death, what if I can't stop the werewolves?" Eugene asked, playing with his shirt.

"You are not alone, Eugene. The weight of this problem does not rest only on your shoulders. Trust the team. They won't let you down." Death looked deep into Eugene's eyes, and he was convinced Death could read thoughts.

"What if I let them down?" That was his biggest fear. He didn't want to let *anyone* down. Not again, and not anymore.

"If you let them down, which you won't, it won't be the first or the last time," Death said with a smile. "You are human, Eugene, and a young one at that. You will disappoint people and let some down. It's the nature of growing. Stop beating yourself up. You moping around is not helping anyone, including yourself."

Eugene straightened his back. "I wasn't moping."

Death crossed his arms and angled his head.

Eugene put his hands out in front of him. "Fine. I was having a pity party. And by the looks of it, the party is over." The last thing he needed was to be known as the moping Intern.

"All you need to do is try, Eugene. As long as you are *trying* to do your best, people will trust you," Death told Eugene.

That sounded way too simple.

The front door to the apartment opened and Eugene turned around. Bob rushed through the door.

"Why are you standing here? You still haven't showered?" Bob asked Eugene.

"Sorry, I was just talking to Death." Eugene told Bob, pointing behind him.

Bob gave him a strange look. "You were, huh?"

Eugene turned to find Death no longer there. "Where did he go?" Eugene asked. "I swear, he was here." Was he going crazy now?

"Relax Eugene. I believe you," Bob told him. "Death does that all the time. It took me a few months to get used to it. Are you feeling better?"

"Actually, I do" Eugene told him in a confident tone. "All I can do is my best. Nothing more, nothing less." He gave Bob a pointed stare, daring him to argue.

"That's all we ever asked of you," Bob said. "And your best is pretty impressive. Why do you think Constantine lets you come back?"

"I thought it was because Death made him," Eugene answered.

"Do you honestly think anyone, including Death, can make Constantine do something he doesn't want to do?" Bob shook his head for added emphasis.

"You have a valid point there," Eugene said "You guys don't mind that I keep losing stuff?" Eugene's voice was a little shaky when he asked.

"Between you and Isis, there is never a dull moment," Bob

admitted. "But enough talk. We need to go soon. Abuelita wants us now." He headed towards the door.

"Do I still have time to shower?" Eugene asked hopefully.

"Oh, you better. I just wiped down Storm," Bob told him. "But make it quick," he said as he stepped out.

"Yes Sir," Eugene told Bob, then he rushed to the bathroom.

Eugene was hoping for a long shower, but that was not an option. He settled for another super-fast shower. When he forced himself to climb out, he threw on a pair of cargo pants and a lose t-shirt, then stepped out of the room. When he walked in the living room, he found Bartholomew inspecting Bob's TV stand.

"Holy crap. What is it with you guys appearing out of the blue?" Eugene told Bartholomew. "First Death tries to give me a heart attack, and now you."

"Sorry, Eugene," Bartholomew said, blushing. "Bob said you were on a tight schedule and I wanted to catch you before you took off," he confessed.

"I'm kidding, Bart. What's going on?" Eugene smiled.

"Bob said you tried to take on a werewolf by yourself," Bartholomew told him.

"Did he tell you how much I sucked?" Eugene's good mood was disappearing.

"No. On the contrary, actually. He said you did pretty well," Bartholomew told Eugene, who was surprised by that comment. "The problem is not you," Bartholomew said, and Eugene gave him a skeptical look. "Not entirely. Yes, you need more training, but you are still dealing with supernatural beings. That means the playing field is not fair."

"Bart, you are not making me feel better," Eugene confessed.

"I know, sorry," Bartholomew said in a hurry. "Here." He gave Eugene a package he had picked up from the couch. Eugene hadn't even noticed it.

"You got me a present," Eugene told him with a hand over his heart.

"I ordered it last night after I saw the results of your fight," Bartholomew told Eugene. Isis had bragged Bartholomew had the best delivery service on the planet. Eugene felt the need to tell Isis that had been an understatement.

"What is it?" Eugene asked Bartholomew as he eyed the box.

"It works better when you open it," Bartholomew told him.

Eugene ripped the box open to find a pair of black combat boots, and some brass knuckles. He pulled the boots out and noticed they were his size.

"Am I getting an Isis uniform?" Isis had more combat boots than most active-duty soldiers. Eugene always admired her boots, but he wasn't sure how they were going to help him today.

"These are better," Bartholomew told him in an excited voice. "Instead of steel toe, you got silver. Same thing with the knuckles. They are silver and coated in wolfsbane." Perfect for knocking out werewolves, or just keeping them away.

"You got these for me?" Eugene wasn't sure if he wanted to hug Bartholomew or cry.

"You are my boy. I can't let you walk around unprotected," Bartholomew told Eugene. "I just wished they had been here earlier," he added.

"Bart, it's perfect right now. Thank you so much," Eugene told him and gave him a fist bump.

"Glad you like it," Bartholomew said with a huge smile. "It won't kill them, but it will give you a fair chance. Okay, I have to get back upstairs. Bob told me to tell you to hurry. Don't be late," he mumbled the last part before running out the door.

"Thanks Bart," Eugene told him again as he took a seat on the couch to change his shoes. He was surprised how much his confidence had risen just by receiving a pair of boots. He wasn't helpless. Even if the werewolves could take him, he was planning to give them hell before they did.

CHAPTER 15

E ugene rode in the truck with Bob in a much better mood. He was feeling a lot more secure and even fearless. He was sure it was an adrenaline high, but he didn't care. His friends didn't hate him and it was okay for him to avoid kids in his experiments. Eugene hadn't realized how many things he'd been worrying about under the surface.

"You look a lot happier," Bob told him as he drove down Highway Eighty-Two towards Abuelitas. Abuelitas was a small Tex-Mex restaurant on Nash, right off the highway. The owner was Abuelita, the coolest grandmother Eugene had ever met. She was around six feet tall, with fabulous silver hair. She was still beautiful for her age. Eugene dreamed of having a grandmother like her. Not to mention he loved her food.

"I feel calmer," Eugene told Bob. "I loved Bartholomew's gifts. I'm also hoping Abuelita has food ready." Eugene was hungry and would take any excuse for a plate of Abuelita's chicken enchiladas.

"It's Abuelitas. Of course there will be food," Bob told him. "The goal would be to not eat so much we end up in a food coma and unable to work." Eugene hated when Bob added reason to his food plans.

"Thanks," Eugene mumbled. "I was ready for the food coma."

"I'm sure you were," Bob told him, shaking his head in amusement. "Did your boots fit?"

"Bartholomew is good. They fit perfectly." Although Eugene had no idea when Bartholomew had checked his shoe size.

"Here, this is for you," Bob told Eugene. "They are Chinese throwing stars, small enough so nobody will notice them. Best part is, they are made of silver."

Eugene ripped the box apart. "Oh wow, these are great," Eugene said as he played with the stars.

"Glad you like them," Bob told Eugene as he pulled into the parking lot of Abuelitas.

"That's weird. The place is empty," Eugene told Bob.

"Abuelita keeps changing her hours. She is only doing dinner on Tuesdays," Bob explained.

They both got out of the truck and walked towards the main entrance. Eugene was afraid what they would find. He was praying Abuelita was fine. If something had happened to Abuelita, he was sure his throwing stars would be getting immediate use. He prepared himself for the worst as Bob opened the door.

"Fourth!" Eugene screamed and rushed inside.

The missing Fourth was sitting with Abuelita, having lunch. Eugene couldn't believe it. Eugene rushed forward and tackled Fourth in a huge hug the poor man was not prepared for.

"What was that for?" Fourth asked as he pulled away from Eugene.

"I have been so worried about you," Eugene told him, trying to keep the tears in check. "Your kidnappers are asking for ransom for you. Constantine is working on a negotiation," he explained, trying not to sound crazy.

"Negotiations?" Fourth almost screamed. "Rookie, you know our rules."

"Yes I know. But this is Death's territory and they have different rules than we do," Eugene told Fourth.

"Eugene is right. City wide genocide is out of the question," Bob added.

"City wide genocide. Bob, please tell me you're kidding?" Abuelita asked him.

"That's Pestilence's rule," Bob told her and no other explanation was needed.

"I knew that heifer was crazy as hell," Abuelita said, appalled. Fourth's eyes got really wide at Abuelita's comment. Bob and Eugene had to turn around to hide their smiles.

"The Mistress is not a heifer," Fourth told Abuelita.

"You are right. I have other chosen words for that one but will leave those for another time," Abuelita told Fourth. "Eugene, honey, are you shrinking to death?" she asked Eugene, her eyebrows scrunched in concern.

"No ma'am. It's probably stress," Eugene told her, trying to sound convincing. He was sure his stomach was eating him from the inside out from hunger.

"I don't believe you. I'm getting you some food," Abuelita told Eugene in a tone that left no room for argument. "Have a seat so you can visit with your friend. Bob, you are eating too, so sit down."

With a shrug of his shoulders, Bob took a seat next to Fourth.

"Thank you, Abuelita," Both Bob and Eugene said in unison.

"My pleasure guys. Get comfortable. Remember the drinks are over by the bar." Abuelita pointed at the drink area as she walked around it to get to the kitchen.

"Will do," Bob responded and stood, moving to the drink area.

Abuelita had the best Horchata in Texarkana. Bob grabbed one for himself and walked to the table with another one.

"Here you go, Eugene." Bob handed him his drink.

"Thank you," Eugene told him grateful Bob had read his mind.

"No problem," Bob said. "So Fourth, where were you? Shorty's people have checked all the hangouts for Los Lobos with no luck," Bob asked, and Eugene was glad. Eugene really wanted to know, probably even more than Bob did.

"They had me in the second floor of the Union Station building Downtown," Fourth told them.

"That building needs a new owner. Too many people just keep using that place to stage their crazy schemes," Bob told Fourth.

"It's a beautiful building if somebody was willing to put in some time and money," Fourth informed them.

"How did you get away?" Eugene asked.

"You would never believe this, but those idiots left this crackhead to watch over me," Fourth told Eugene in disgust.

"They literally left a crackhead or just an odd guy?" Bob asked Fourth, leaning on the table.

"I wished it was lack of option but no, he was definitely an addict," Fourth confirmed.

"I'm still not following you. How did you get away?" Eugene asked Fourth.

"Easy, I convinced the poor fool to try some of the drugs they left behind." Fourth puffed out his chest.

"That easy?" Eugene couldn't believe it. Compared to his last twenty-four hours, Fourth had just been chilling.

"Of course not," Fourth clarified. "I had to take some first before he would try it. It wasn't his fault really. Leaving an addict next to a container of drugs is like leaving a kid at Toys-R-Us and expecting them not touch anything."

"Here you go, boys." Abuelita walked in carrying two large plates. "Make sure to eat everything." She gave Bob and Eugene a pointed stare.

"Thank you, Abuelita," Eugene told her, ready to dig in.

"Looks and smells amazing," Bob said, sniffing the steam rising from his plate.

"My pleasure. I brought you some to-go boxes to take with you," Abuelita told them.

Eugene was really happy since now he didn't have to feel guilty that Second was missing out.

"You are awesome Abuelita. Thank you," Eugene told her with a soft smile.

"Okay Fourth, back to you," Bob told him.

"What happened to the crackhead watching you?" Eugene asked, realizing he had no idea if he was still alive.

"I left him on the floor," Fourth said in a calm tone.

"You left him to die?" Eugene asked him.

"Of course not, he was just passed out," Fourth said, leaning back in his seat.

"Fourth, you do remember we didn't dilute that batch?" Eugene asked Fourth. "You realize that sample you gave that boy was pure."

"Oops," Fourth said. "I'm sure he is okay. Or else my new little friend will be meeting your boss soon." He directed the last part at Bob.

"How come the drugs didn't have the same effect on you?" Abuelita asked Fourth.

"We are immune to all sorts of drugs, poison, and chemicals," Fourth told Abuelita with a smile.

"Well that's convenient," Abuelita told him. "Unless you boys need me, I'm going to start getting ready for my dinner crowd." She left the three men with their plates and headed to the kitchen.

"How did you get here?" Eugene turned back to Fourth.

"I walked," Fourth told him. "It was a lot farther away than I expected. I was planning to walk all the way to Reapers but saw Abuelita coming in with boxes. I couldn't resist and decided to help her. She offered to call you guys instead of me having to walk the rest of the way." He went back to his food.

"We are glad you are okay," Bob told Fourth.

Now that Fourth was safe, Eugene had no idea what the next step would be. When his phone rang, he was grateful for the interruption.

"Hi, Rookie. Everything okay?" Second asked when Eugene answered the phone.

"Everything is perfect," Eugene told him. "You would never guess who we found."

"Besides Abuelita, I have no idea," Second told Eugene.

"Then hold on to something because you are not going to believe this," Eugene told him. "We found Fourth. Actually, Fourth found us but the result is the same."

"You were right; I don't believe it," Second admitted.

"We will be heading back shortly. Please let Constantine know," Eugene told Second.

"Not a problem. See you soon," Second told Eugene and they both disconnected.

"Now what?" Eugene asked Bob.

"Sounds like a question for the boss," Bob answered. "Which means we need to get going."

Before they could get up, Abuelita came rushing out with bags of food.

"Here you go. Have a great rest of your day, and get those punks," Abuelita told them as she patted the top of their heads.

"Thank you again, Abuelita. We will keep you posted," Bob told her as he stepped toward the door, ushering Eugene and the other Intern out in front of him.

It felt wrong heading home with Fourth after all the problems his drugs were causing. Eugene would just have to ask Constantine for some advice.

CHAPTER 16

Eugene couldn't believe it, but after twenty four hours of stressing and worrying, it was over. Something wasn't right. The situation felt anticlimactic.

"Are you okay?" Bob asked Eugene as he was pulling into his parking space at Reapers.

Eugene shrugged "Yeah, I guess."

"So this is the famous Reapers?" Fourth said from the backseat. "It is definitely deceiving from the outside. Not bad." He climbed out of the truck.

"Let's go, Eugene. You need some hot chocolate," Bob said.

Eugene couldn't help but smile as he followed Bob, dragging Fourth with him.

They didn't make it too far in the loft when Fourth was tackled by Second. Eugene had to jump out of the way to avoid getting crushed by the excited man. He never realized how much Second cared about Fourth.

"Fourth, you are alive. I'm so happy," Second told Fourth, still holding him tight. "Now give me my five hundred bucks before you get yourself kidnapped again."

"I knew I liked that one for a reason," Constantine told Bob, who started laughing.

Fourth struggled to get to his pocket, but managed to pull his wallet out. He handed Second five Benjamins and Second released him.

"Thank you," Second told Fourth, kissing his money. "Welcome home my little friends. I have missed you." He cradled his money to his cheek, and when he noticed everyone watching him, he shoved it in his pocket and moved to the dining table.

"Let me guess, the man doesn't pay?" Bob asked Second.

"Oh, he pays, but on his own time and never the full amount,"

Second clarified.

"I thought Pestilence at least paid well," Constantine added.

"According to her records, she pays almost as much as we do," Bartholomew told Constantine from his computer station.

"How much?" Constantine asked as curious as any cat over shiny objects.

"About forty-five hundred a month, not counting lodging, food, clothes, and utilities that are all covered." Bartholomew was reading from his screen.

"How do you know all that?" Fourth asked, almost disgusted.

"He knows everything," Eugene told his peers. "Don't get offended. He could tell you a lot more if you asked."

"Who cares how Bartholomew found out? The real questions is, what do you do with all your money?" Constantine continued his interrogation.

"Gambling problem," Eugene tried to whisper, but it sounded like a scream in the quiet room.

"Traitor," Fourth told Eugene.

"Just helping you out," Eugene told Fourth. "Things go a lot smoother and faster if you don't lie." Not that Fourth would ever admit anything, but Constantine had a knack for finding the truth, one way or another.

"Now that makes sense," Constantine said in a matter of fact tone, but there was no judgement there. "What do you guys play?"

Eugene giggled. Constantine's curiosity was getting the best of him. Eugene could tell he was trying to control himself but was having too much fun to stop.

"UNO," Second answered after a few minutes.

"UNO?" Bob asked from the stove. He had moved to his kitchen while everyone was talking. He had milk on the stove and was taking out ingredients from the pantry.

"Don't hate on UNO," Second told Bob.

"It's a better competitive game, full of strategies," Fourth added.

"Especially if you are drunk and can't think straight," Eugene translated for Bob.

"How is that possible?" Bartholomew asked. "Wouldn't your immunity stop you from getting drunk?"

"You have to drink a lot of liquor and very fast, but it can happen," Eugene explained. "By the time you are done, you are more stuffed than drunk. But it makes for a fun night." He added a smile.

"Sorry Eugene, that doesn't sound fun at all," Bartholomew told Eugene, shaking his head.

"I agree with Bartholomew. Too much work for very little results," Constantine told Eugene.

"We are very grateful for your hospitality, but it's time for us to go," Fourth told the Reapers team. "I need a shower and a nap." He rubbed his stomach.

"We can fix both of those things," Bob told Fourth, putting Abuelita's food on plates for everyone else.

Fourth didn't answer Bob, although he watched him very closely. Bob handed Bartholomew, Constantine, and Second their lunches, then went back to the fridge and grabbed a pie.

"Have a seat Fourth, please," Bob said, carrying the plate to the table. Fourth walked over and took a seat. "You should join him as well, Second. I'm pretty sure you guys don't eat too well at the lab." Bob placed another plate in front of Second.

"It's pretty good, just not as good as yours." Since Eugene was the resident expert that got to visit both locations, he felt confident in his assessment.

"Thank you, Eugene, that makes me feel better," Bob admitted to the guys.

"Thank you, Bob," Second told Bob as he started devouring his food.

"Oh wow. This *is* amazing. I never tasted anything so good," Fourth told Bob. "Did you really make this?"

"Bob can do miracles with the simplest ingredients," Constantine told the two men as they ate.

"This is delicious, but as soon as we are done, we need to get home," Fourth told the room.

"We are leaving?" Eugene asked Fourth.

"Of course. We no longer have business here," Fourth told him. "Not to mention we have been away from the lab for too long." His tone was serious. Eugene wasn't happy, but what could he do? Fourth outranked him.

"What about the werewolves?" Second asked.

"What about them?" Fourth shot back.

"Are we just going to let them keep passing our formula around? People will start dying soon if we don't stop them," Eugene said, trying to keep his voice normal.

"Why do we care?" Fourth responded, not an ounce of concern in his tone. "So what if a few people die? It doesn't affect us."

Eugene pressed his lips together. He needed a better approach. It was obvious Fourth didn't care about the citizens of Texarkana.

"I just didn't think we were going to let them go unpunished," Eugene said, trying to sound uninterested. "It's not like our reputation is at stake here." It was his last gamble, but he had a feeling Fourth would bite if his pride was involved.

"What do you mean?" Fourth asked, and the words came out hesitant.

"Oh, you know the routine. If you let one group of punk kids walk all over you, the rest of them think they can do it anytime." Constantine explained, and as Fourth looked at the ceiling in thought, Constantine winked at Eugene.

Eugene tried to hide his smile.

"If the Mistress finds out somebody stole from us and blackmailed us, she will be pissed," Second jumped in. "I think we need to teach those assholes a lesson."

"Good news, we already have a meeting set up for tonight at nine," Constantine told them. "I'm sure if we work together, we can come up with a great ambush." His words came out so cheerful it worried Eugene. The crazy cat had to be planning something big.

"Why would you want to help us?" Fourth asked, a bit skeptical.

"Easy. We are all related here," Constantine explained. "If people think they can take advantage of one Horseman, they will try it with the rest. I can't afford to have Death mad. It isn't a pretty sight. So, it's in our best interest to take care of this problem as soon as possible." Constantine planted a huge smile on his face, showing his canines.

No doubt about it. The cat was smooth, and it amazed Eugene just how smooth he was.

"I second the motion," Second said and then laughed at his own words. "I been waiting ages to use that phrase. Second has seconded the motion." Eugene covered his face while Constantine rolled his eyes. "I also have a drone we can use to recon the area."

"What can your drone do?" Constantine asked in a flat tone.

"You know, the usual," Second said, trying to sound modest. Eugene knew the drone was Second's pride and joy. "Aerial maneuvers, video and audio recording, as well as still images." He grinned.

"Not bad," Constantine said. "Mine has missiles, machines guns, and can be controlled from here for over a hundred-mile radius." Constantine angled his head, waiting for a comeback.

"Okay, you win," Second conceded, bowing down.

"I told you he was a smart one," Constantine bragged to Bob, using his head to point at Second.

"This is all great, but what are we going to do?" Fourth asked the group.

"We can set up some traps in the area before the meeting," Bob told them.

"They are werewolves. They will be able to smell your scent in the air," Fourth said, crushing everyone's dreams.

"We can create a smell neutralizer," Eugene told them. "The devil did it for me when he sent me out to chase those lunatics." Which he was still mad about. The devil's trickery wouldn't go unpunished, though. He had plans to get him back one day.

"That's a great start," Constantine remarked, his tone pleased.

"Where is the meeting point?" Eugene asked.

"In Wake Village, inside King Baseball Park," Bob informed the group.

"Not the most ideal location, but at least it's outside," Fourth said. "We can make a few potions for our new friends." He drummed his fingers together, which made him look more than diabolical.

"Rookie, do you have enough stuff here to make some weapons," Second asked Eugene.

"We probably have a little of everything, but we'll need a lot more," Eugene replied.

"We could send Shorty back to your lab to get the supplies while we do the recon," Bob told the group.

"I like the plan, but there's a small problem," Fourth told them.

"What?" Constantine asked, his whiskers twitching in confusion.

"Me!" shouted Fourth.

"I don't get it. What about you?" Constantine replied.

"He is supposed to be kidnapped," Bartholomew said as he got closer to the kitchen table.

"Not a problem at all," Constantine said to Fourth. "You stay here so that way the area is not contaminated."

"That sounds great, but why would they agree to the meeting if they don't have me."

"Easy. They don't know you are here," Constantine said. "We will play it off like we are still looking for you so nobody gets suspicious."

"Basically, we continue searching and go to this meeting like we don't know anything," Bartholomew added.

"Exactly," Constantine said, giving Bartholomew a proud look.

"Looks like we got some shopping to do," Bob told the group, then he handed everyone a mug of hot chocolate.

"You better get going. We don't have a lot of time," Constantine told them.

"We are going to inspect the lab," Eugene said as he headed towards the door. Bob, Second, and Fourth followed closely behind, while Bartholomew and Constantine went to the computer area.

CHAPTER 17

Eugene left Second and Fourth at Reapers since they were working on a few tonics for the werewolves. Their experimenting had produced some pretty neat tricks the wolves would never see coming. Bob had made several trips to the lab to ensure they had everything they needed.

They had even a few FaceTime chats with Seventh to get pointers on their new techniques.   He was so eager to help, and Eugene couldn't have been more surprised. He'd never had this much support from his mentors.

Needless to say, the goal had shifted. He didn't care about the werewolves disrespecting his team any longer. He cared about not letting people down, showing his people that he could keep it together and make them proud.

Reapers was well equipped and at times it had better supplies than his own lab. Eugene was sure that was all Bartholomew's doing. Unfortunately, with three scientists working non-stop, even Bartholomew had a hard time keeping up with the stock. He needed canisters, Fourth needed bug repellent, and Second was short on gummy bears. Eugene decided it was safer not too ask about the last one. Sometimes, when it came to his peeps, ignorance was bliss.

When Bob volunteered to go on the shopping run, Eugene went with him. He was having a great time bonding with his people, but after hours of it, Eugene was burnt out. Bob drove them to Academy's. According to Bob, he had a few items he needed as well.

They drove in silence to the store. Not an uncomfortable silence, but the kind of silence enjoyed with a great friend. Bob also had an uncanny ability to give people space when they needed it, which Eugene was more than thankful for right then.

"Do you think this is a bad idea?" Eugene asked Bob when they pulled in a parking space.

"They need to be stopped and nobody else can do it but us," Bob told Eugene before turning the truck off.

"I'm asking all of you to risk your life to do this. I want them to pay for what they did to those kids and what they are doing to the town, but I don't want any of my friends to get hurt in the process."

"Would you prefer if we walk away and let them run amuck?" Bob asked. "Eugene, they know where to find you. They know the stuff you guys can make. Now that they got a taste of power, they are not going to stop."

Eugene was processing Bob's words when Shorty came to a screeching stop next to them.

"He is a menace. You know that, right?" Eugene said right before Shorty got out of the truck.

"Oh, trust me, I know," Bob told Eugene. "I tried to stop the boss, but you know Constantine. Once his mind is made up, there is no going back. Good news, though. Under careful supervision, Shorty is a huge asset." Bob got out of his truck and Eugene followed suit.

Shorty had the Triplets in tow and they looked ready for war. The Triplets all wore green camouflage while Shorty had a matching set in black. Shorty even sported a black bandana, making him look like a small Ice Cube.

"Big Bob, it's almost time!" Shorty told Bob. "We need to teach those punks a lesson." At his words, the Triplets nodded like bobble-head dolls.

"You were saying, Eugene?" Bob asked Eugene with a smirk.

"Do you really think this a good idea?" Eugene asked again.

Shorty's eyes widened. "E, we can't let people run all over us. It's about time we go on the offensive and lay down the law," Shorty told him, and the Triplets mumbled sounds of agreements.

"Shorty, Los Lobos are an abnormally large pack. People could get hurt." Which was his biggest worry. Eugene had no idea what it would take to handle a pack of werewolves, but he had a feeling they didn't have the manpower.

"News flash, E. People are already getting hurt. Some have died, and even more will if we don't stop them." Shorty planted his hands on his hips and jutted his chin out.

"Shorty has a point. Too many people have been hurt already and we can't keep running around stabbing people with meds to help them," Bob told Eugene. "Besides, this was your plan. Don't get cold feet now."

"I know. I'm just afraid we don't have enough people to handle this," Eugene admitted, his biggest fear being voiced. "With their numbers, this is going to be a suicide mission."

"Don't even worry. We got this," Shorty told Eugene before he turned to the Triplets. "You know what to do."

"You got it, Boss," the three replied in unison, then they took off, but each went a different direction.

"You do know that is really creepy." Eugene pointed at the Triplets. "What exactly are they going to do? And why do they look like the pirates in the first *Pirates of the Caribbean* movie?" His eyes stayed on the Triplets, sure all they needed was to morph into skeletons and they would look identical to the characters in the movie.

"Don't judge. You said we needed people, so they are going to recruit," Shorty told him.

"Do we really know people crazy enough to join us?" Eugene asked, starting to wonder what kind of recruitment power Shorty had.

"Crazy? Never," Bob told him. "What we have is a lot of people looking for a purpose. Defending their town is as good as any." His tone sounded sure, and when his chest puffed out, he looked more than confident.

"People problem fixed. Now what?" Shorty asked.

"We got some shopping to do," Eugene told Shorty.

"Here. This is your list," Bob told Shorty as he gave him a piece of paper with a long list of items.

"Why do I get a list?" Shorty asked Bob, his eyes on the paper.

"Because you are here and we need to hurry. Unless you have other stuff to do today?" Bob asked Shorty, giving him a hard look.

Eugene had to giggle. Bob was the only person who could intimidate Shorty. Well, maybe Constantine, too, but he wasn't here. And when Shorty didn't reply, Eugene knew it was because he didn't have a job other than working for Reapers.

"Hey, sacrifices have to be made for the good of the team," Shorty announced, trying to sound humble.

"Glad you could spare us a minute. Let's go," Bob told Shorty and took off towards the store.

"Do you think Big Bob is going to feed us before the big event?"

Shorty whispered to Eugene. "It's not right to head to battle on an empty stomach."

"That is a really good question," Eugene told Shorty, even though he didn't want to admit he was already hungry again. "I hope he does. I would hate to get my ass kicked *and* be starving to death."

"Oh good, glad we agree on that," Shorty told Eugene and walked a bit faster to catch up with Bob. "Hey Big Bob, E has something he wants to ask you," Shorty shouted across the parking lot.

"What is it Eugene?" Bob asked without slowing down. Eugene had visions of choking Shorty in the parking lot.

"Oh nothing really. Just wondering if we could have dinner before going to war," Eugene told him, trying to sound nonchalant about it.

"Of course." Bob said like it was the most obvious thing in the world. "I got two lasagnas in the oven now. Hence the reason we must hurry. I don't want them to burn." He moved a little faster.

"What? Why didn't you say that before?" Shorty told Bob and took off at a full sprint.

Eugene couldn't believe it. He had never seen Shorty run, definitely never at a full sprint. He was a fast little guy for his age. Eugene had to jog to keep up with both men. Shorty was on a mission from God. The food God, at least. That man would do anything for food.

With Shorty's new inspiration, the shopping adventure at Academy's took less than thirty minutes. They each had a shopping cart packed with stuff. Bob had given Eugene another list, too. He had no clue what Bob had planned, but they bought everything from nets, to grills, to all sorts of fishing gear, and even hunting equipment. This was the strangest war Eugene had ever been a part of. Then again, he had never been to war in his life. The extent of his experience with violence came from being bullied at school, but that stopped after he nailed the bullies' lockers with stinky bombs. Nobody could ever prove it had been him, but the kids knew he had done it, which made him the new nerd super hero. Nobody messed with him after that.

"We need mines," Eugene told Bob as they passed each other in one of the aisles.

"Way ahead of you," Bob told him, grabbing a couple of rat traps.

"What are we going to do with those?" Eugene asked, nudging his head towards the traps.

"Fourth is planning to adjust them so when they step on them, a strong sleeping gas will be released, Bob said with a wicked grin.

"Sleep gas or nerve agent? It is Fourth we are talking about," Eugene asked, his tone filled with concern.

"Just sleep. Constantine explained to him, twice, how killing them was out of the question," Bob told Eugene.

"Did he listen?" Eugene knew how stubborn Fourth could be.

"Only after Constantine explained that any deaths caused by their tricks would have to be explained and reported to Death," Bob said with a grin. "He also added that Fourth would be the one doing the reporting."

"Ouch. That's low, even for Constantine." Eugene felt sorry for Fourth.

"Low, but also effective," Bob said. "Are you done? We need to go." He looked over his list again.

"I got one more thing," Eugene told Bob and took off to find sunscreen. He had no idea what they were planning to do with that, but at this rate, he didn't care.

In no time, they were at the register paying for all their stuff. The poor cashier wasn't sure what to say about their diverse purchases. Bob paid with Reapers' business card. Isis had told Eugene they had unlimited credit on their cards and everyone had one. Eugene was grateful for it, since it expedited their shopping process.

When they finished, they almost ran out of the store. Time was of the essence and they didn't have much left, so they needed to get back as soon as possible.

CHAPTER 18

Reapers was buzzing with excitement. The Triplets had done an amazing job recruiting and there were people everywhere, although it made Eugene wonder what they had been offered to show up.

Someone had rearranged it to accommodate the new influx of people. The gym had become Bob's command center, and he'd tacked up a map of the park and the surrounding area. Captains were assigned per location, and each group was given a small platoon of troops. Eugene had never been in the military but he was pretty sure this was how they ran missions.

Bob did "rock drills" with each platoon to make sure they knew what they were doing. Eugene had no clue what a rock drill was, though it looked more like role playing. Bob would place each person in their location, and they would simulate their movements like it was a real attack. It impressed him, but it also confused him. How could anyone remember all those moves? He had no idea how Bob was doing it because he remembered all their moves, plus traps they had set up way earlier.

But according to Constantine, the werewolves were going to scout the place as well, so their traps had to be well concealed.

Bartholomew was busy as well. He was in the lab that was back to being the arms room, issuing specific weapons to each platoon. The sharp shooters were with Bob, being placed on the roofs of the buildings near the park. They'd practiced before they went in the shooting range, using a long-range simulation program. Hopefully that prepared them, otherwise it could lead to Eugene being a potential friendly-fire target.

Everyone had a job this evening. Constantine was working with Second and Fourth in their assembly line. They were spraying each person down with their version of scent eliminator. Constantine had the pleasure of inspecting. According to Constantine, his sense of smell was five times more accurate, and even stronger than the werewolves. That was really scary since a normal cat could already smell fourteen times stronger than a human. Wolves' sense of smell was about one hundred times stronger. Eugene did the math in his head. If all the facts he had were true, Constantine could smell a person at least three miles away.

"Why do you look constipated over there?" Constantine asked Eugene.

"I'm still processing how accurate your sense of smell is," Eugene admitted.

"Don't. It will blow your mind *and* give you a headache," Constantine told him. "Fortunately for me, that gift didn't come all at once or I would have passed out. Thankfully, I'm able to control it now. Living in this confined space with a bunch of humans could get disgusting fast." He scrunched his nose up.

"I don't know if I ever want to imagine that." Chills ran down Eugene's arms. The idea of smelling every body odor, every release of gas…it made him shudder. It also made him want to puke.

"Breathe, child. It is too early for you to be passing out," Constantine told him. "By the way, what are you supposed to be doing?" He narrowed his eyes at Eugene.

"Shorty and I are supposed to be the ones delivering the goods, since they know me and all. Bob sent me over here to get ready," Eugene explained.

"We got less than forty-five minutes and your plan for getting ready is standing around." Constantine's mouth fell open and he shook his head. "Boy, get your ass in that room and go get changed," he growled.

"Change into what?" Eugene asked as he scrunched his forehead and looked around.

"I don't care. Superman, Batman, or Shaft. You name it, just pick one. But you are not going outside to a show down representing us while you look like that." Constantine pointed at Eugene's lab coat.

Eugene *was* pretty dirty. He had stains all over his jacket and his hands were covered in some strange-looking blue slim. Luckily there wasn't a mirror around. He had a feeling his face looked even worse.

"Eugene, we got this assembly under control. Go shower and get ready. You are the face of this operation," Constantine told him.

"We left you clothes and some gear in your room. Hurry up."

Eugene felt a little lost, out of place, and like he wasn't pulling his weight. Unfortunately, he knew Constantine was right. Eugene had seen Isis get ready for a mission, and her appearance played as much of a role as her skills. Isis looked like a cross between Lara Croft and Trinity from *The Matrix*. That thought gave him a brilliant idea: he was going to be Morpheus, or maybe Blade. It didn't matter which, he just needed to look smooth and lethal. Eugene ran to his room to shower with a new focus.

Bob's apartment was loud. Eugene had no idea who was playing music, but Barry White screamed from the speaker system. With a smile, he ran to his room, then headed for the bathroom, but he stopped in his tracks when he spotted the clothes Constantine had left on his bed.

Eugene had no words. He had expected a suit, but this was the suit of a life time. It was a custom made William Westmacott Ultimate Bespoke. That little number was over seventy-five-thousand dollars. Eugene was afraid to get closer until he spotted a pair of House of Testoni shoes. Last time he checked, the starting price for those babies was thirty thousand. Not the most practical shoes for battling werewolves, but he sure looked good.

Eugene sucked in a breath. His clothes had to cost more than some houses in Texas. Eugene had an admiration for classic suits and great shoes, but he never thought he would have the opportunity to wear one. Isis had mentioned Constantine had more money than God and the most expensive taste in the world. She hadn't been kidding. Forget Morpheus or Blade, Eugene was going to be channeling his inner Bond—James Bond that was.

"Yes!" Eugene shouted to himself. "If I'm going down, at least I'm going to do it in style." Excitement quickened his steps as he rushed to the bathroom. He couldn't wait to try on his clothes. This had to be a dream and he was living it.

Eugene stepped out of the apartment at eight forty looking like royalty. He even walked with a swagger that would put most models to shame. Reapers was deserted, except for the regular residents.

Bartholomew stood next to Bob, Constantine, and Shorty, and his eyes found Eugene first. The boy genius let out a long whistle.

"Looking fly, E." Shorty told him. He was also wearing an expensive suit, just not to the level of Eugene's.

"Feeling fly, Shorty," Eugene replied. "You are looking pretty stylish yourself."

Shorty grinned, then they gave each other a high five.

"I told you I knew about measurements," Bartholomew told Constantine.

"Not bad. Not bad at all." Constantine was sitting on top of the DeathMobile. That was Isis's name for Death's Mustang. It was hard to say if it was greenish, yellow, or just a pale puke color. The description of Death's horse from the book of Revelation came to him, and he grinned. Nobody could say Death didn't have a sense of humor.

"One more time. Shorty, you will be driving Eugene in the DeathMobile," Bob said, jolting Eugene out of his thoughts.

"What? Are you crazy?" Eugene shouted.

"Eugene, you are representing the Horsemen. They need to know we are a unified front," Constantine said. "What better way to make a statement than to have one of Pestilence's Interns arrive in Death's horse? It's all about symbolism, baby." He grinned like the mad hatter.

"Shorty, if you put a scratch on this baby, we are both dead," Eugene told Shorty as serious as he could.

"Oh trust me, E. We are driving down there like this car is in a funeral parade. I'm not taking any chances," Shorty told Eugene.

Eugene took a couple of deep breaths, then prayed Shorty had meant what he'd said and could at least follow his own instructions.

"Okay, Eugene, turn around. Let's take a look at you," Constantine told him. Eugene did a slow turn and everyone admired him. "Perfect."

"You got your guns?" Bob asked Eugene. He opened his jacket to reveal two 9mms inside a custom-made holster that blended with his suit. With a nod, Bob continued. "Now you are ready. You have enough tranquilizers to take out three of them easily. When things go wild, you two get in the car and get out. Got it?"

Both Eugene and Shorty nodded in agreement.

"Time to go. I'll be your eyes in the sky from the Command Center. Give those fools hell," Constantine told the group and took off.

"We will be in position by the time you get there," Bob told them.

"Bob, wait. Where are Second and Fourth?" Eugene asked, expecting to find his peers before he left.

"They are already in place," Bob told him.

"What? Why? They are not fighters," Eugene replied a little louder than he expected.

"No, they are not, but they are part of this team," Bob told Eugene. "They refused to stay behind knowing you were on the front line risking everything. Now, we got to go," Bob told him and rushed to his truck.

Eugene's lip quivered as emotions hit him straight in the feels. He hadn't expected all these people to put everything on the line for him, but they had and he couldn't have been more grateful.

"Hey, Eugene. The suit and shoes are not just fabulous, they are also super practical," Bartholomew whispered. "Shoes have silver plating in them, and the suit is the same material as Isis's uniform. It will take a bullet and even spells," he said with a wink. "Must hurry before Bob leaves me." He waved as he ran towards Bob's truck.

"Bart, you are the best," Eugene shouted at Bartholomew.

"I know," Bartholomew replied with a smirk.

"Are you ready to make those punk pay?" Shorty asked Eugene.

"It will be my pleasure," Eugene replied and they both climbed in the DeathMobile.

CHAPTER 19

Shorty drove unusually slow to the park. Eugene was glad that Shorty had some boundaries. Death's vehicle was the one-line Shorty was not willing to cross. Eugene thanked God for that. He didn't want Death to rip his soul apart for damaging his car.

Wake Village's baseball park was not that far from Reapers. They were at the location in less than eight minutes. Eugene was expecting to be nervous, but instead a strange calmness settled over him. Maybe it was the calm before the storm. He didn't care. He was focused and ready for battle.

Shorty pulled into the parking lot of the park to find several trucks and cars already there. Fortunately, the city wasn't having any games, or this little meeting would turn into a massacre.

Shorty parked as far away from all the other vehicles. "Here comes Big Bob," he told Eugene.

"It's show time," Eugene told Shorty. "Whatever happens, it's been an honor working with you, Shorty. Thank you."

"E, please. This is not our funeral, so no need for speeches," Shorty told Eugene. "Save the pretty words for our furry friends over there." He pointed to the pitcher's mound where four werewolves stood.

"Let's go," Eugene told Shorty.

The men stepped out of the car looking as smooth as Bond. Eugene strolled towards the pitcher's mound with Shorty acting as his body guard. Eugene had to admit, they looked really good. They reached the mound and faced off with their enemies. There were three huge males and the angry female.

"Impressive. You clean up well, little one," the female told Eugene.

His cheeks heated. He hated to admit it, even in his own head, but the female was stunning. "Business attire, what can I say?"

Eugene said in a calm tone. "Let's not waste any time. Where is my colleague?"

"What? No small talk?" the female asked. "Aren't you going to tell me how we are going to regret this?"

"It seems you already know, so no need to restate it," Eugene answered with a smile.

"Oh please, you really don't think the Horsemen will come to your aid. You are alone, little boy, and we are running this show," the female told Eugene.

"You and three linebackers are running things? Somehow, I highly doubt that," Eugene told her. "Tell me, *little girl*, who is the leader of this pack. I don't want to waste my time talking to underlings." He played with his watch for extra emphasis.

"Underling? You will pay for that. I run this pack," the female told him.

He responded with a raised eyebrow. Then, he kept his expression as bored as possible as he said, "Good for you. Who did you have to kill to get the job? I doubt your pack believes in equal opportunity programs."

"My brother," the female answered. "That should tell you something. If I'm willing to kill my own family, getting rid of you won't be an issue." Hatred glimmered from her eyes as she stared at Eugene.

"We weren't expecting loyalty among your group," Eugene told her, trying to add as much anger to his voice. He was trying to get her mad to reveal the rest of her pack. "Should we get this started, little Loba, or do you need to wait for the full moon." Luckily, there wouldn't be a full moon. He'd checked earlier. The last thing he needed was extra help for the other side when they already had a huge advantage.

"You talk a big game, but you will still pay our price." The female smiled and let out a high-pitched whistle to her pack.

From the visitor's side, two huge men dragged a hooded figured to the field. The man was dressed identical to Fourth, which meant one thing: they were never planning to release Fourth. Not when they already had someone ready for the switch.

The two giants stopped next to their leader, dropping the fake Fourth in the middle.

"Take the hood off. I want to verify he is not hurt," Eugene told the pack.

"Not until we get our loot," the leader told him. "I'm not taking any chances. For all we know, you're passing secret messages with your group and setting us up." She eyed Eugene.

"Shorty, call for the packages," Eugene told Shorty.

Shorty pulled out his phone and made a quick call. Constantine had warned everyone about werewolves hearing, so Shorty didn't even bother whispering. Bob and the Triplets climbed out of the truck and walked to the bed of the vehicle. Bob had two large wooden boxes in the back. Bob and one of the Triplets grabbed one of the boxes, the other two Triplets carried the second. They moved quickly around the field and stood next to Eugene and Shorty.

"Packages," Eugene said, pointing to the really large boxes. "Now my colleague." He pointed at the fake Fourth.

"Not so fast," the leader said. "I hope you don't get offended that I don't trust you, but let me see the goods. Open the boxes." She waited patiently for the guys.

Bob looked at Eugene.

"Go ahead," Eugene said like a true boss. He was having a blast playing the part, but the game was about to come to end.

Bob popped the lid to the first box. The Interns had delivered. The top of the container was powerful heroine cut with cocaine and rat poising.

"Hope you don't mind if we test it?" the leader asked.

"You don't get near my stash until I get my colleague," Eugene told her.

"In that case, at least let us check the other box. Open the lid," she demanded.

Eugene was starting to hate her more and more. "If you wish. This is my present to you, with love," Eugene said in a condescending voice, then he walked with a swagger to the other box and opened it.

Eugene didn't bother to look at Bob because he knew this part of the drill well. He stood to the side and popped the lid. Unfortunately for the little werewolves, instead of another trunk full of drugs, it was only carrying a fully loaded Bartholomew. Bartholomew opened fire on the werewolves as soon as the lid allowed him. Second had made a new compound to diminish the speed and strength of the werewolves.

"You are going to die," screamed the leader as she was covered with Bartholomew's compound. "Kill them," she ordered her packed.

The linebackers next to her started shifting. The transformation was slow and even painful to watch. Whatever compound Fourth made had added an extra bonus. As soon as the werewolves shifted to their wolf form, all the fur fell off them.

"Oh damn," Eugene told Bartholomew as they watched the full transformation. "I don't think that was supposed to happen."

Horror filled Bartholomew's features as he took in the wolves as they twisted in pain right in front of them.

"No!" the leader screamed, watching her bald wolves. "Now!" She howled to the rest of her pack.

Eugene had no idea where they came from, but over forty werewolves surrounded them. Some were in men form, others in their wolf form, and a couple were still in between. Those were extremely scary because they had human legs with the upper body of a wolf. Not a good look at all.

"Our turn now!" Bob gave the order and all hell broke loose.

Over eighty men and women came charging up the field. From the rooftops, the snipers were taking out any wolf that got too close to Eugene. Bartholomew had jumped out of his box and was shooting at every wolf he found. Within seconds, hair littered the field. Eugene took out his guns and fired at everything. No way would he take any chances. Unfortunately, he was so distracted by the two wolves on his left that he missed the leader sneaking up on his right.

"I should have killed you when I had the chance," she told Eugene, grabbing him by the neck.

Eugene struggled to get out of her grasp, but all he managed to do was turn himself around and face her. She wasn't shifting to her wolf self, probably to avoid the same fate as her people. She still had super strength, and sharp claws that dug into him.

"You have sentenced your colleague and yourself to death," the leader told Eugene, showing him the most pointed canines he had ever seen.

"Sorry, little lady, not today," Eugene told her and landed the best punch ever.

The leader doubled down in pain, staring at Eugene with shock. With a smile, Eugene showed her his hand, exposing the silver knuckles Bartholomew had given him. And he'd nailed the punch. It made him so happy he wanted to dance. He didn't have time to celebrate, though. Another wolf instantly charged at him. Without thinking too much, Eugene turned around and landed a kick to the wolf man's groin. It sounded like something broke, and Eugene prayed it hadn't been his testicles. No man deserved that fate.

"Oh. God," the werewolf mumbled, cupping himself as he collapsed to the ground.

"My bad," Eugene said. He hadn't walked into this with the intention of killing anyone, or destroying their manhood, but if it happened, not much he could do. Instead of inspecting the damage, Eugene rushed over to help the rest of the team.

Constantine's drone hovered over them, but since everyone was on top of each other, he couldn't get a clear shot.

Shorty was helping the Triplets tackle one large wolf. It took six men and women to take him down. Second and Fourth joined the fight and were spraying the wolves with a sleep formula. The wolves were so strong, it was taking multiple shots for the formula to take them out.

Screams were heard all over the park, but no sense in worrying about that because Shorty had people to make sure no civilians came in. It also ensured none of the wolves escaped, so two birds with one stone kind of deal.

Platoons worked together on the large wolves. They used everything they had available to them, from rifles and clubs, to baseball bats and sticks. A couple of the team members were taken down by a wolf, their arms and legs broken in the process. Bob had created a true army. When one of their team went down, four people jumped in to save him. Men were rushed off the field for medical treatment and more came in to back them up. Nets were thrown from trees and traps in the ground were activated. Werewolves were pushed in every direction, separating them from their pack. The wolves were dominated.

The fighting did not take long—maybe twenty minutes. The Reaper team had taken control of the situation and Bob's plan had been executed well.

It helped that the wolves had underestimated them. Eugene had noticed some staggering and unable to shift properly. They had been drunk. But it didn't matter because it only helped the team. Every small victory was a big one in his book. When the last wolf fell, he was hit with more sleeping compound.

"Last one secured, Big Bob," one of the Triplets announced.

"Great job everyone." Bob said.

"What do we do with them now?" Bartholomew asked.

"We will take care of that," Fourth told him. "We need help taking them back to our lab."

"What are we going to do with them?" Eugene asked.

"We can't have a group of wild shifters attacking people and disrespecting the Horsemen," Second told him. "You know the restricted level?" Eugene shook his head. He didn't have access to the seventh level, but he'd always wanted to know what they did there. "That's where we take our more serious experiments. Some brainwashing will be in order." Second smiled wickedly.

"Remind me not to piss you guys off," Bob told Eugene.

"Me too," Eugene told him. "I don't know what that level is, but it sounds scary." He didn't like the idea of brainwashing anyone, but he also didn't like the idea of letting the wolves go wild either, so it was definitely the better option.

"So, how do we move forty people to Hope?" Fourth asked as his gaze roamed over the comatose werewolves.

"It might take several trips, but we can do it," Bob told them. "We will need one of you guys on the trucks to make sure none of them wakes up while in transit. Let's get started."

It was going to be a long night.

CHAPTER 20

Eugene was amazed how long it took them to transport all the werewolves to the lab. Even with Shorty driving one of the vehicles, it took the team six trips back and forth. That was the easy part. Once all the werewolves were in the lab, moving them to the sub levels took even longer. All the werewolves had to be secured in stretchers. Their clothes had to be changed. IVs had to be connected, and only then could the new patients be moved to a secure chamber.

The werewolves were left under the care of Ninth. Eugene had always wondered what their senior Intern did all day. After watching him in the strange lab/hospital area, he didn't want to know. He was sure this was a scene straight out of the *X-Files*. Seventh had told him they'd have to make some memory modifications, then they would apply behavior enhancements, but Eugene refused to ask any questions. He didn't want to know, and he hoped by the time he reached this level of access, what was done there would no longer be a requirement.

Unfortunately, it was ten in the morning by the time Eugene made it back to Reapers with the team. Second and Fourth had stayed at the lab to clean up and rest. Fifth had informed everyone that due to all their shenanigans during the week, they were behind with their drug making for the Fourth of July party. Eugene was supposed to return for the company car and get back to work ASAP.

He didn't argue. He knew he hadn't been pulling his weight all week and that the Mistress wanted an awesome event. Seventh interceded on Eugene's behalf and told Fifth all the party favors were done. Eugene had no idea how the old man did it, but they were actually ahead of schedule in production.

With Eighth and Ninth busy with their new guests, Seventh was the senior member on staff. His word was the law, and he gave all the Interns the day off. Fifth was appalled until he realized that meant him as well. He took off running to binge on the BBCs *Sherlock Holmes* series. Fifth was addicted to Netflix. Eugene was given leave to swing by Reapers, pick up the hearse, and return to work in the morning.

As he was heading out, Seventh told him how proud of him he was, which put Eugene on cloud nine. It was probably the reason he was still smiling as he crashed on the leather couch at Reapers. It was a good day. Nobody had died. Very few people were seriously hurt. The werewolves were contained. To make the day even better, he didn't have to go to the club for the party.

Eugene couldn't be happier

"Has anybody seen Shorty?" Bartholomew asked the group.

Most of the people in the room looked dead. They were barely moving. Bartholomew sat at his computer, resting his head on the desk. Bob had curled up on one of the dining room chairs. In fact, the only one awake was Constantine, and he was wiping his face with his paws on top of the kitchen island.

"He is moonlighting for Seventh," Eugene told Bartholomew.

"Doing what?" Bartholomew asked, his forehead scrunched.

"He is our new transporter," Eugene told him. "Well, him and the Triplets. After Seventh saw them, he decided they were a much more intimidating group of people than any of us put together."

"That is actually a really good idea," Constantine told him. "It would be a sad day in hell for anyone who messes with that group." He had moved to clean his legs when the door flew open.

"I did it!" Isis came in the room cheering at the top of her lungs.

"It's about time you get back," Constantine said in greeting.

"Weren't you supposed to be back Friday?" Bob asked as he raised his head from the table.

"I was able to convince my little stubborn ghost to leave," Isis told everyone, smiling from ear to ear.

"You got him to move on to his next life?" Constantine asked, raising an eyebrow at her in that strange way the wrestler "The Rock" used to do.

"I wish," Isis replied, and Constantine frowned. "Relax. Let me explain. It seems my new favorite soul lived a horrible life and he wanted to make atonement now. He wants to warn the living of the consequences for their sins. Regardless, I convinced him to move to the bed and breakfast and leave the little house alone. That way he would have a better crowd." She chuckled.

"That's pretty smooth, Isis," Eugene told her. Her eyes darted every which way before Eugene realized she couldn't see him because of the way the couch faced.

"Eugene, why are you not at the lab?" she asked when he finally stood up. "And why are you all dressed up?"

"It's the Fourth of July party, so the Mistress gave us the day off," Eugene explained. It wasn't a total lie, though. It had been Seventh that gave them the day off.

"I didn't realize Pestilence was that patriotic? What about the clothes?" Isis asked, crossing her arms over her chest.

"We were LARPing," Bartholomew jumped in to save Eugene.

"As what, *Mission Impossible*?" Isis asked, raising an eyebrow.

"More like Bond, you know, *From Russia with Love*," Eugene said with a smile. The rest of the guys nodded in agreement, even Constantine.

"Well, I'm proud of all of you. But I recommend a shower now," Isis told them. "You all smell like wet dogs" She scrunched up her nose. "No offense Constantine."

"None taken," Constantine told her. "They do reek to all bloody hell." He wiped his whiskers.

"I'm off to bed. I had a very long couple of days," Isis told the boys. "By the looks of you guys, you all did too. See you for dinner," she told them and headed towards her room.

"She has a point. I recommend you all head for the shower and then bed," Constantine told them. "I'll hold down the fort."

Eugene didn't need to be told twice, and nobody else did either. Everyone moved at once, but they took their time.

"Hey Eugene," Constantine said before Eugene walked out the door behind Bob. "Not bad for a rookie. Nice job." Constantine wasn't known for empty compliments, so this meant a lot to Eugene. "Nice to have you in the family."

"Thank you, Constantine," Eugene said with a huge smile on his face.

It was a really good day after all. Now he just needed a shower and some sleep, then life would be perfect.

Fall in love with the action packed series The Intern Diaries from the very beginning with book 1, Death's Intern at www.amazon.com/author/dcgomez

For up to date promotions and release dates of upcoming books,
sign up for the latest news here:

Author Page: www.dcgomez-author.com

www.bookbug.com/author-d-c-gomez

www.Facebook.com/dcgomez.author

www.Instagram.com/dc.gomez

www.goodreads.com/dcgomez

ACKNOWLEDGEMENTS

I would like to start by thanking YOU! Thank you for reading this book and taking this wild journey with me. You are the reason to wake up each day, to create stories that will delight you.

A huge thanks goes to my incredible support system, who continue to cheer me on each day. Thank you to my family and my better half for supporting me even when my dreams are all over the place. Thanks to my community, who continue to support me beyond all my dreams.

Many thanks goes to a very special angel that continues to blow my mind with her talent and passion, the talented Cassandra Fear. Thank you for being the most supportive editor and an amazing cover designer. Thank you to the fabulous and talented Ms. Courtney Shockey, formatter extraordinaire. Thank you for putting all the pieces together and giving me a product ready to publish.

Absolutely, it takes a village to get this done. I'm so grateful for all everyone I meet that makes this journey so exciting each day. Happy Reading.

ABOUT THE AUTHOR

D. C. Gomez was born in the Dominican Republic and at the age of ten moved with her family to Salem, Massachusetts. After eight years in the magical "Witch City," she moved to New York City to attend college. D. C. enrolled at New York University to study film and television. In her junior year of college, she had an epiphany. She was young, naive, and knew nothing about the world or people.

In an effort to expand her horizons and be able to create stories about humanity, she joined the US Army. She proudly served for four years. Those experiences shaped her life. Her quirky, and sometimes morbid, sense of humor was developed. She has a love for those who served and the families that support them. She currently lives in the quaint city of Wake Village, Texas, with her furry roommate, Chincha.

This is the 6 x 9 Basic Template. Paste your manuscript into this template or simply start typing. Delete this text prior to use.